PRAISE F

Death Comes To Hawbury is cosy crime at its finest. The characters are memorable, the mystery is tightly plotted and there is at least one sentence per paragraph that is laugh out loud funny. More, please!

— CHRIS MCDONALD - AUTHOR OF THE
STONEBRIDGE MYSTERIES

I've found my new favourite cozy crime series! Verity and Leeanne are amazing! Lots of laughs throughout. LOVED IT!

— S. GRIFFITHS

Witty, well-observed and great fun. Perfect for readers of the Agatha Raisin series.

— H. WATSON

DEATH COMES TO HAWBURY

A VERITY MEADOWS MYSTERY

A J FORD

For Bird
My real-life partner in crime.
There's no me without you.
Love always

x

Verity Meadows stood outside what had once been her upmarket Kensington home, wrangling a small herd of wayward removal men and fighting off tears.

As the removal men exited the house, she checked their cargo against a multi-page list, before directing them between two removal vans. The contents of the large van—mostly original art and fine furniture—was destined to be auctioned at Bonhams. The small van—mostly handbags and cheese-boards, as far as she could tell—was heading for a new home in the country, which all sounded rather grand until you actually saw the cottage, which was, to use estate-agent speak, "nestled" between a defunct tyre garage and a dried-up duck pond in a place called Hawbury, which according to Wikipedia had once boasted the title of "England's fifteenth tidiest village". As far as Hawbury's location on a map, Verity believed it lay somewhere between Bristol and the back of beyond.

For many city dwellers, escaping to the countryside was the dream, but not for Verity. Unfortunately, she'd been left with no alternative, thanks to her former accountant and newest member of Interpol's 'Most Wanted', Marcus Pickering, who had embezzled the better part of three million pounds from Verity and her husband. Marcus had last been seen boarding a one-way flight to the Dominican Republic, with a Gucci carry-on bag in one hand, and a Z-list celebrity slattern in the other.

Verity couldn't allow herself to dwell on what that swine had done to them, as it was very likely to bring on a prolonged bout of swearing and kicking things. Instead, she channelled her pent-up emotions into motivating the flagging workforce, many of whom were muttering variously about tea breaks, trade unions, and human rights lawyers.

The new owners of the house, Mr and Mrs Damien Wade-Peller, were waiting opposite in their silver Bentley, ready to jump in Verity's grave the second she vacated the property. They were accompanied by a sullen-looking child—a teenage girl with blue hair and matching temperament.

Verity pretended not to notice them, but she'd seen them alright: him, checking his watch or wrestling with a copy of the *Financial Times*, her, inspecting her make-up in the vanity mirror or checking the tension of the skin on her neck. Emo was listening to music through headphones that looked heavy enough to break her pencil-thin neck. The last time Verity had looked in their direction, the girl had pressed her middle finger squarely against the window. The instant Verity saw this she directed her eyes skyward, as though she'd seen something shoot overhead, to prevent the obnoxious brat from reading her lips.

The vans were loaded and on the road at a few minutes past one. Verity watched them drive away before walking through the house on the pretence of checking that nothing had been left behind. In reality, she was saying goodbye to the place and thanking it for a multitude of fond memories.

The click of the latch as the front door closed behind her pierced her heart. She pressed her palm against the door and closed her eyes, as though in silent prayer. *Thank you.*

'Ahem.'

Verity came back to the present. The Wade Hyphen Sodding Peller family stood before her. Mr Wade-Peller held out his right hand, palm up.

'Key,' he said. A command, not a request.

'Oh, yes. Sorry.' Verity began to remove the front door key from her key fob. As she pulled the key free from the ring, she noticed she was standing very near a storm drain. She thought about the satisfying sound the key would make if she were to drop it through the grating, before surrendering it. He held her gaze for an uncomfortable second before snapping his hand shut. No thanks were forthcoming.

'All keys should have been surrendered to the estate agent,' he said.

'I know. I'm sorry. These are my husband's spare keys and he's away on business. It completely slipped my mind that I had them.'

'I'm sure it did,' he said contemptuously. 'Much like the fact that you and your property should have been out of our house before midday.' Ordinarily, Verity would have taken the bait and fired back at him, but she was too emotionally drained to get into a row with this pompous prat.

'Right,' she said. 'I suppose that's it, then?'

'Yes, it is. Goodbye,' he said, before joining his family at the front door of their new home. Verity walked to her car. She'd taken only a few paces before she stopped and turned back. 'Excuse me,' she said. The Wade-Pellers stood in a tight cluster in the doorway, waiting for Verity to speak, all three looking quite put out.

'Sorry. Just to let you know that the shower basin in the master en suite leaks, so you might want to get a plumber in.'

Mr Wade-Peller gave an exasperated sigh. 'You could have mentioned this sooner.'

'Yes, you're quite right. And you could have paid somewhere near our asking price.'

The un-Botoxed parts of Mrs Wade-Peller's face creased at this remark.

'How dare you speak to my husband like that!'

'Oh, go and iron your neck!'

'Have you *quite* finished?' Mr Wade-Peller said, through clenched teeth.

The girl was clearly enjoying seeing someone stick it to her parents and was struggling to suppress a smirk.

Verity was feeling quite spirited now. Confident that she had the child's attention, she upped her game. 'Nearly. I'm not sure if the estate agent has mentioned this, but we believe the house is haunted by the ghost of a little girl, so you might want to get a priest in while you're at it.'

The child's expression changed from one of undisguised satisfaction to a look of abject horror in an instant.

'Right, I think that covers everything,' said Verity, as she got into her car. 'Good luck.' As she drove away, she gave the traumatised trio a convincing smile, somehow managing to hold back her tears until she was some distance down the road.

Hawbury was one of the lesser-known villages that surrounded the picturesque town of Brenton. The area had been designated an Area of Outstanding Natural Beauty, thanks to its endless rolling hills and sweeping meadows. Ancient fields formed a patchwork of pastoral scenes: rustic farmhouses were set amongst golden wheat fields; bucolic stone cottages lined meandering country lanes, barely wide enough in parts for a brace of bicycles; a whitewashed water-mill sat at a crossroads, its wheel lapping languidly at a shallow stream. You could drop a landscape painter more or less anywhere in Brenton, spin them around a few times, and fully expect them to paint a masterpiece based on what they saw before them.

All of this was largely wasted on Verity, however. Yes, it was all very pretty, there was no disputing that, but as far as she was concerned, the countryside represented the absence of essential amenities and an abundance of inconvenience, and was best appreciated at a distance—preferably in the form of a calendar or a postcard.

As Verity neared the village, the weather deteriorated.

So much for endless blue skies, she thought, as a flotilla of grey rain clouds closed in on the village at a rate of knots. An unreliable satnav signal meant that Verity was forced to rely on her own hastily jotted notes for directions. She almost missed the welcome sign she'd been looking out for, as it was partially obscured by a teenage boy in obscenely low-slung jeans and a black hoodie. He was frantically scrubbing at a section of spray paint, under the scrutiny of a sturdy and fear-some-looking red-haired woman. The sign had previously read, "Welcome to Hawbury. Visit once and die happy." Some wit—presumably the boy in the hoodie—had sprayed over the word "happy" and tagged his work with a crude biological drawing.

Once past the sign, she had driven on for a mile or so when the heavens finally opened, and rain came down in

5

biblical proportions. She was approaching a narrow stone bridge, the windscreen wipers operating at full speed, when a tractor came over the horizon, bearing down on her. She braked hard, causing the car to skid into a hedgerow. Verity winced as thorny twigs sought to make their mark in the paintwork.

'Arse!' she said, thumping the empty seat beside her. She squinted through the windscreen, trying to determine the tractor driver's intentions, but it was difficult to see the tractor, let alone its driver. She sighed and lowered her side window. By means of frantic arm waving and shouting, she tried to encourage the tractor driver to reverse. He responded with a definite shrug and a shake of the head. It was clear that it was she who would have to concede. Cursing, she closed her window to prevent any more rain getting in, or any colourful language getting out, and tentatively reversed down the narrow lane, all the time the tractor advancing toward her. She turned into a passing place, braking abruptly when she heard the crunch of plastic. Oblivious, the tractor driver passed her, holding up his hand when he was alongside. Furious, Verity returned a variety of hand signals, none of which were to be found in the Highway Code, and drove away at speed.

The rain had eased when she reached their new home. The cottage was a chocolate box thatch. It had originally been built in the first quarter of the eighteenth century as a one up, one down "squatter's cottage", though it had been extended in subsequent centuries. It stood behind a tired picket fence, and was enveloped by an overgrown garden dominated by climbing roses. The exterior of the cottage was similarly neglected, with a distinct patch of thinning thatch and paint flaking off warped window frames. One of the upstairs windowpanes had fallen victim to a well-struck cricket ball from the nearby pavilion, leaving a section of yellowing net curtain desperately trying to escape from the jagged glass maw. The cottage had been bequeathed to Verity by her mother's sister, who had passed away the previous year. The fact that she was the only beneficiary of her aunt's will came as a complete surprise to Verity, as the pair hadn't spent any real time together for the best part of thirty years, though they had once been very close, during Verity's formative years. Since she had left for university at the age of seventeen, the only communication between Verity and her aunt had been the exchange of Christmas and birthday cards, in which every year Aunt Dorothy would extend an invitation to Verity and 'that gorgeous man' of hers to visit, and every year Verity pledged that they would do so, just as soon as they were able to find the time. Inevitably, time eventually ran out, and Verity finally made good on her promise when her aunt's body was commended to its final resting place. Looking at the cottage now, and recalling her childhood visits to the village, Verity made another pledge—one she would not fail to make good on: the minute they were back on their feet, and this place had been brought back to its former glory, she'd sell it and they would be back in London before the ink had dried on the paperwork.

2

When Verity recalled the incident, much later, she believed it was the plasterer's incessant whistling that pushed her over the edge. After six weeks in their new home, most of the essential repairs had been carried out: the thatched roof had been repaired, broken windowpanes replaced, rotten joists had been made good, and the lounge and kitchen ceilings had been patched up, so the place was, if nothing else, now watertight. Throughout it all, Verity had managed to tune out the whining of power tools and constant hammering. She'd even tolerated their choice of radio station, which allegedly played "all the hits, all the time". But that man's whistling was sent to test her, and it was a test she had failed in spectacular fashion. By the morning of the third day she was ready for him.

'Morning, missus. Lovely morning for it.'

If by "it" he meant murder, she couldn't agree more.

'Indeed,' she replied, as she finished washing up her breakfast things. She caught herself wringing the life out of an innocent dishcloth and set it down. Without prompting, she filled the kettle and put a flame under it, reasoning that listening to someone slurping tea wasn't half as bad as being subjected to the whistling of a tone-deaf clot with a missing front incisor.

The plasterer was working in the lounge, standing on his plastering rig—a scaffold plank set between two paint-spattered beer bottle crates—ready to apply a skim coat to the ceiling. Verity was well-versed in his routine. She stood in the kitchen, primed and ready to strike.

He'd managed to mangle half a bar of 'I Do Like to be Beside the Seaside' when she jumped out from behind the door, brandishing a washing-up brush, business end first.

She glared at the workman, with murderous intent. 'One more whistle out of you, sunshine, and I'll—' The kettle came to the boil and began to whistle, tunelessly. Two pairs of eyes swivelled in its direction.

Mercifully, at that precise moment the front door opened, and the plasterer's young apprentice walked in, unable to wipe his feet but successfully managing to avoid the dust sheets his colleague had just laid out.

The plasterer, who held his arms aloft like the victim of an active armed robbery, was evidently relieved to see the youth. 'Thank God you're here. I'm pretty sure she was intent on doing me a mischief with that brush.'

The apprentice set down a plastic bucket full of plastering tools and tried to make sense of the scene. 'Everything alright?'

The timely interruption was sufficient to allow Verity to regain some of her composure. 'Yes. Perfectly fine, thank you.' She lowered the washing-up brush, returned to the kitchen and took the kettle off the heat.

Realising that she might be a little tense, she decided that it would be a good idea to take a stroll through the village for a couple of hours to unwind. 'I'm going out. I may be some time. If you manage to finish before I get back—and, please, for all our sakes, try to—close the door behind you, I've got my keys.' She took a navy trench coat off the coat stand and threw it on over her "slobs"—leggings, and a pullover with a bleach stain down the front—before stepping into a pair of ballet pumps and leaving through the front door.

She'd travelled perhaps twenty yards down the path when she heard the plumber kick off a torturous rendition of 'We Wish You a Merry Christmas', evidently oblivious to the fact that it was June. She gave a short shriek and quickened her pace.

Despite Verity's numerous reservations about the move, she could not deny that the village had a certain "quintessential English charm". The buildings in the centre of the village were an eclectic mix of single and two-storey honey-hued lime-stone cottages, topped with lichen and moss-encrusted slate roofs or dark thatch. These were interspersed with the occa-sional twisted Jacobean timber-framed building. A weathered medieval stone cross stood in the centre of the crossroads. There was a row of terraced shops—mostly boutiques and tea rooms, their fronts bedecked with an abundance of pendulous wisteria flowers, which emanated from a single, gnarled trunk. Faded pastel bunting was strung in a zig-zag fashion across the street, suspended in perpetuity, in preparation for the next village fete or parade.

Verity was new enough to the village that she still walked around with her head on a swivel, in an effort to identify the few shops she might visit more than once—other than to ask the whereabouts of the shops that sold things she actually wanted. She reasoned that there were only so many Hawbury

tea towels that a Hawbury resident would need in one life-time, and if pushed to declare precisely how many that might be, she suspected that the answer fell somewhere between zero and none.

She thought about stopping in one of the tea shops but, given the fine weather and the day's influx of tourists, the like-lihood of finding a vacant table was remote. Considering this, she remembered just how much she missed the familiarity of the chain coffee shops that littered the streets of London. Once, during a brief exchange with a woman in the queue at the bakery, Verity made the mistake of suggesting that a Star-bucks would "do a bomb" in the village. The woman reacted as though she'd been stung and made it clear that if anyone were brave enough to open a chain store in the village, the bomb Verity had mentioned was likely to be of the very real exploding variety. Realising that the Luddites still held sway in Hawbury, and sensing that the aggrieved woman was building up a head of steam, Verity created a diversion by reacting to an imaginary wasp, and made good her escape.

After spending some time wandering aimlessly, Verity found herself standing next to the Hawbury Parish Council notice board. She scanned it with interest. The variety of activities taking place in Hawbury over the coming week were dizzying. There were the ubiquitous slimming and Zumba classes, which were held weekly in the community centre. Lost Pet posters—mostly cats, and a parrot called Rasputin. The WI were offering baking classes, which caught Verity's eye. The local am-dram society, The Hawbury Players, were hosting a murder mystery evening at Hawbury Manor. The meeting of the Golden Age Writers' Society was cancelled due to illness. The list went on: Hot Yoga classes, Latin Ballroom Dance, Clay Pigeon Shooting. The Psychic Night with Graham Garfield, Pamela George, and Madame Crystale Rose,

who would "bring to you their unique abilities and talents, from readings via tarot cards, crystal ball, mediumship, angel cards as well as pure psychic connection with your loved ones in the spirit world."

Despite the promise of excitement and amusement on offer, the one notice that commanded Verity's attention the most was a small notice under the heading "Job Vacancies".

3

Less than twenty-four hours after spotting the vacancy, Verity was on the way to a job interview at the parish council offices, which were in The Old Courthouse. It was for the position of Parish Clerk, which, from what Verity could make out from the job description, was essentially an office manager—a role she'd excelled at for many years, prior to starting her own business. It was a part-time position, with exact working hours and schedule to be agreed. The pro-rata salary was a fraction over twenty thousand pounds per annum, which was hardly going to set their world on fire, but it would help. But this wasn't about the money, this was about getting back to her old self. It would also be a fantastic opportunity to integrate into the community, which was something of a closed circle.

Verity had attempted to do some preparatory research the previous evening, but the Hawbury Parish Council website hadn't been updated in over three years, and she'd gleaned nothing from the Twitter account, @hawbury, other than the fact that the eradication of dog fouling was a top priority. This

meant she would be going into the interview woefully under-prepared by her usual standards. She had learned that The Old Courthouse was built in the 1880s, in a Tudor Gothic style, and it had once served as both the police station and petty sessional court—a fact that came in handy when it came to finding the building, as this designation had been carved into the stonework above the entrance. Verity pulled up outside the building when she saw the double yellow lines, which ran the length of the street. Her interview was scheduled for midday, and it was already a quarter to twelve. Flustered, she scanned her surroundings for a parking space. After a moment, she saw a stone archway at the side of the court-house and a sign with a P and an arrow above it. Hopeful, she turned into the entrance, only to be forced to slam on her brakes as an arse of a man in an Audi cut across her path and shot through the archway at perilous speed, narrowly missing the stonework. Her blood was up now. She followed him into the car park, determined to get a parking space and give him a piece of her mind while she was at it.

Adrenaline surging, she accelerated hard, stone spraying in her wake. The car park was near capacity, and she could see the Audi driver making his way past a row of parked cars. Verity spotted a vacant parking space.

'More haste and less speed, matey,' she said as she headed for the space. As she did so, he'd reached the end of the row of parked cars. He'd seen the same space, too. They were approaching each other now, head on. Wordlessly, both drivers had consented to a game of chicken. *Game on.* Both floored their accelerator. Gravel shot out in a deadly arc, and dust rose as the tyres of the two prestige vehicles desperately fought to gain traction. The cars bore down on each other. Closer now, perilously so, the drivers glared at one other. The solitary parking space had become something both were

seemingly willing to die for. It was the Audi driver who conceded, braking violently as his nemesis threw her Mercedes into the space. By some miracle, her car stopped a scant inch from the surrounding cars. Verity gave a triumphant roar before slumping forward onto the steering wheel, her heart racing and legs shaking. In retrospect, she probably should have dealt with that differently. After a moment of breathing exercises, she sat up and looked at the clock on the dashboard. 11:52. Hands still shaking, she reached into the passenger footwell to retrieve her handbag and a pair of classy black heels. She slipped on the shoes and exited her vehicle. The Audi driver hadn't moved; his car had stalled at an awkward angle, the front bumper a few inches off a lamppost, and the rear of the car had narrowly missed a cast iron downpipe. Seeing the woman get out of her car, the Audi driver hastily leapt out of his vehicle, determined to tear a strip off her.

'What are you playing at, you silly cow?' he said. 'You very nearly killed me then!'

Verity turned to him. 'Excuse me? I very nearly killed you? You nearly took the front of my car off when you pulled into here, you lardy pillock!'

He was clearly taken aback. 'How dare you speak to me like that! Do you know who I am?'

'No, I don't. But I know your type, alright. You're an arrogant tosser with an over-inflated sense of importance in his pants. But guess what, buster, I saw this parking space first, and you bloody well know it, so suck it up, buttercup!' She was about to turn away, satisfied that she'd put this ox into his place, when she found herself jabbing a finger in his direction, her mouth racing to catch up. 'And if you even think of touching me or my car, I'll hunt you down and kill you. Understood?'

The man stood stock-still and slack-jawed. Shocked and secretly delighted by her outburst, Verity turned her back to him and crunched awkwardly across the gravel toward the side of the courthouse, not daring to turn back.

Verity reported in to a receptionist at the front desk, which doubled up as a tourist information point. A small Perspex stand held a few assorted guides and leaflets, many of which were one or two years out of date. After being directed to take a seat in the corridor on the second floor, Verity thanked the receptionist and picked up one of the leaflets. It had the tantalising title: "Top Eight Things to See in Hawbury". Verity had never seen a "Top Eight" list before.

She sat on one of three blue seats which lined an oak-panelled corridor and glanced up at a wall clock that appeared to have been installed shortly after the courthouse had been constructed. Then she checked her watch. She'd made it with two minutes to spare. *Not tardy*, she reminded herself, *punctual*.

She had started to read the leaflet when a door to her right opened and a woman in a bright, hand-knitted jumper and large, purple spectacles appeared and addressed her.

'Hi. Are you...' she looked at the sheet of paper in her hand, 'Ms Meadows?'

Verity put the leaflet down and stood up, holding out her hand. 'Mrs Meadows, yes. Hi,' she said, giving a winning smile. The woman's outfit was enough to induce sensory overload; buttons, beads, bangles, and bracelets—a riot of contrasting colours and textures, not unlike a seventies Christmas tree, Verity thought.

The woman stepped out into the corridor, wiping the fingers of her right hand on the leg of her burgundy corduroy trousers. 'Excuse my fingers, I've just had a cheeky packet of Cheetos. You have to eat it while you can in this place.' Verity took her tarnished hand very briefly and shook it with considerably less vigour than she usually would.

'I'm Leeanne—one word, not two. We're running a bit behind, actually, so would you like a cup of tea or...' She let the end of the question fade to silence.

'...or coffee?' Verity suggested, hopefully.

'No. Would you like a cup of tea or not? I was supposed to call into McGee's to get some coffee on the way in this morning, but my cat had left a dead bird on the mat. His name's Elvis—the cat, not the bird. I don't know what the bird is called. I don't even know if birds have names.'

'Hmm,' said Verity, approximating a thoughtful nod.

Leeanne opened the next door along, which appeared to be a staff restroom. It was furnished with a couple of scuffed, black leather armchairs, which positively reeked of the 80s, and a dark oak table, which reeked of the 1880s. Around the table stood an eclectic mix of dining chairs. The kitchen area consisted of a small sink and drainer, a kettle, toaster, microwave, and an under-the-counter fridge. Leeanne picked up two mugs from the draining board and sniffed them. The second mug warranted three sniffs. She clicked the kettle on and removed the lid from a caddy labelled 'Coffee' and plucked out two teabags with powdery orange fingers. The teabags were also sniffed before being dropped into the mugs. Verity made a mental note that the mug belonging to the "World's Greatest Dad" had been subjected to the most sniffs.

'Do you take sugar in tea?'

'Yes, please. Just the one.'

Leeanne pulled the lid off the tea caddy, lifted her glasses, and peered inside it.

'Oh. Is sugar a deal breaker for you?'

'No, honestly, it's fine. I'll take it as it comes.'

'Are you sure? I could pour some hot water in here and

swish it about for you—you'll probably get a bit of coffee then, too,' she said brightly.

'No, I'm good, thanks.'

The pair stood in silence for a few seconds. Leeanne looked out of the small window above the sink and gave a contented sigh. She began to drum her fingers lightly upon the worktop before glancing over at the kettle only to snap her head violently away from it. 'Oops.'

Concerned, Verity asked her if she was okay.

Leeanne answered without turning to face Verity. 'I'm fine. It's just that my nanna—Nanna Jenkins, not my other nanna— she's dead. She said that a watched pot never boils, and a kettle is like a pot, isn't it, so…' She trailed off, another sentence dying prematurely on her lips.

The kettle came up to boil and clicked off. 'Could you pass me the milk, please?'

'Sure,' Verity said, and went down on her haunches to open the fridge. The interior light wasn't working, which under normal circumstances might have made the ready identification of the contents challenging but, given the pong which emanated from the small white box, she assumed it contained a job lot of iffy Stilton.

She scanned the gloomy interior of the fridge, careful not to inhale. There was no milk in the door compartment; instead, this held a plastic beaker, which contained either a kale smoothie or algae, and a clear plastic bag which appeared to contain someone's medication, which consisted of a blue plastic box and a couple of syringes. The contents of the shelves were more typical of a communal fridge in a workplace: a tub of low-fat spread, a wet bag of salad leaves, a dimpled kiwi fruit, and several plastic lunchboxes containing a variety of sandwiches. Helpfully, these were labelled with sticky notes and strips of torn notepaper. The labels denoted ownership, rather than contents: "Karina's—Paws off!", "Property of Brian B. Touch this and die" and the haunting, but beautifully inscribed warning, "I sneezed on this."

Verity spotted the milk as the last of her oxygen was depleted. She deftly whipped out the small jug of semi-skimmed, slammed the fridge shut hard enough to rattle some hidden cutlery, and surfaced for air.

Their tea made, Leeanne and Verity sat down at the table, opposite one another. Leeanne took a sip of tea. Verity had set aside the "World's Greatest Dad" mug, hoping she would be able to get away without drinking it. She glanced at her watch. It was now ten minutes past her allotted interview slot. They certainly did things at a different pace in the countryside.

Leeanne got the conversation going.

'So how did you end up living in Hawbury?'

'My husband and I had always planned to retire to the countryside, and a few years ago I inherited property in the village. We had a bit of a setback with our business recently, and, long story short, we decided to make the move.'

Leeanne nodded. 'Okay. Tell me a bit more about your company.'

'It's a property development company, mainly focused on commercial property overseas.'

Leeanne frowned and picked up the CV, flipping it over.

'I thought it said you run a publishing company?'

'Yes, I do, but that's not much more than a hobby, really.'

'So, what is it you publish?'

'It's a series of detective novels my grandmother wrote in the thirties. It's just a passion project, really.'

'That sounds nice. Tell me about this property company then,' said Leeanne.

'It's a property development company, as I said. My husband and I started it about fourteen years ago. After about eighteen months, the business really started to take off. Fast forward to last year, and the business had grown to the point where we needed someone in to help with the day-to-day running of the company, and help take the business to the next level, so we brought in a friend who'd run several successful businesses himself. Over the next six months, Marcus—the friend—was doing some fantastic things with the business. Our quarterly figures were better than ever. Everything was going brilliantly. So, just before my husband's fiftieth birthday, I decided the time was right for us to finally take a proper break, so I booked a surprise two-week holiday in the Maldives, as a special treat for his big birthday.' Verity pulled a tissue out of the sleeve of her blouse and dabbed it under her eyes before continuing. 'Shortly before we were due to fly home, we went for a meal to this fantastic restaurant, it's actually a few metres under the sea—you sit in this clear glass tunnel, and you can see all the fish around you—it's absolutely incredible. Anyway, I went to pay for the meal and my card was declined, so I tried the business credit card and that was declined too. Finally, I tried the business debit card. Same. And, right then, I knew what had happened.'

Leeanne was leaning forward, gripped by this tale. 'Ooh. What had happened?'

Verity blinked away tears and had another dab with the tissue. 'Marcus had cleared out our bank accounts and maxed out all the cards he had access to. And, as an extra special cherry on top, when we got home, we discovered that he'd been rather creative with our accounts, and we actually owed the tax man a significant amount of money, so we had to sell our house to settle the bills and, well, here we are.'

Verity had assumed the question would come up, but she hadn't expected to be so forthcoming. She took it as a sign that she was trying to unburden herself of its weight.

'Wow,' Leeanne said as she sank back into her chair. 'That's unbelievable.'

'Right?'

'Yeah. I've always wanted to go to the Maldives. What's it like?'

Despite Verity baring her soul, Leeanne had completely missed the point. To her surprise, Verity let out a short laugh. 'In my experience, Leeanne, I'd say it was very, very expensive.'

'I thought it would be. I had a meal under the sea, once, but it wasn't in a restaurant. Me and my boyfriend, Gary, were on holiday this one time, and we'd bought fish and chips from a fish and chip shop, but it started raining so we went into one of those fish museums—the ones which have sharks in and that, and you can walk through the tunnels. Anyway, we had our fish and chips stuffed inside our jackets and my boyfriend, Gary, was eating a big piece of fish and the sharks came right up close to us. Gary said he reckoned it was because they could smell the fish. It was amazing. But we got kicked out because Gary tried to pinch a starfish for me.'

Verity was grinning from ear to ear. 'Leeanne. I've met a lot of people in my time, and I can say without fear of contradiction, you are absolutely unique.'

Leeanne gave a bashful smile. 'Thanks.'

Verity glanced at her watch. 12:15.

'Can I just ask if this is the actual interview, and are we still expecting someone else to join us?'

Leeanne looked shocked. 'Oh no. This isn't the interview. Mr Donahue and Mr Henley do the interviews. I'm just the woman who makes the tea and coffee—well, just the tea at the moment—and I help out around the office. To be honest, I'm just being a bit of a nosy cow. I hope you don't mind?'

Before Verity could respond, the door opened and a well-presented man in his early forties strode in, startling the two women. He wore tan shoes, smart jeans, and a dark blue blazer over a crisp light blue shirt, and he wore them well. A signet ring and expensive wristwatch complemented his outfit perfectly.

'Ah, there you are,' he said, approaching the table. Verity stood to greet him, and the pair shook hands. Close up, he was undeniably good looking, with dark hair, bright green eyes, a natural tan, and an easy smile. 'Hi. I'm Tony. I'm the executive officer here. I take it you're here about the parish clerk position. Verity, isn't it?'

'Yes, that's right.'

'Great. I'm sorry to have kept you. I got caught in one of those endless meetings with the top brass, and you can imagine what fun that was,' he said, giving an exaggerated yawn.

Verity gave a polite chuckle.

'Sorry. Leeanne, have you seen Carl?' he asked.

'Well, he was in this morning for a bit, then he said had to pop home for something—he didn't say what—and I haven't seen him since.'

'Hmm. Odd. His car is in the car park. Anyway, not to worry. Why don't we go on through to my office and we'll get proceedings underway?'

Verity suddenly felt very uneasy about this.

Tony's office was the one that Leeanne had first appeared from. There was very little in the way of furniture. Two desks, back to back, two ergonomic desk chairs and a couple of additional chairs, which looked to have been brought in from the staff room to accommodate the interviews. Tony sat at the desk and invited Verity to sit down in the chair opposite. Leeanne took a pen and spiral-bound notepad off the desk, dragged a chair over to a neutral position, and sat down.

Verity could see two copies of her CV on the desk. Tony picked one up and scanned it.

'Hmm,' he said, nodding approvingly now and then, as though he were considering the wine menu in a fancy restaurant. He placed the CV on the desk and sat back in his chair. 'So, Verity, would you like to start by telling us a little about yourself?'

No sooner had Verity processed his question than the door to the room burst open and crashed into the wall, shaking the room. Verity flinched, and covered her head, half-expecting the roof to fall in on her. Leeanne stumbled over her chair in an effort to escape the intruder. Two picture frames containing print-it-yourself certificates toppled off a bookshelf. Tony was already half-way under the desk before the looming shadow of the intruder had reached him.

'You murderer!' a familiar voice boomed. Verity was now on the other side of the desk, brandishing Tony's ergonomic chair like a lion tamer. The familiar voice belonged to a familiar face.

'Are you alright, Mr Donahue?' asked Leeanne.

Verity groaned. The Arse in The Audi and Donahue were one and the same, but the man that stood before her now was the polar opposite of the speechless bully boy she'd confronted earlier. This man was a lunatic.

Leeanne tried to break through the man's mania. 'Mr Donahue? Would you like a cup of tea, or...'

Donahue didn't register he'd even heard her. His attention was solely on Verity, his eyes wide, his lips pulled back in a snarl, baring dirty teeth. He tilted his head back and sniffed the air. If there had been a full moon, she wouldn't have been at all surprised if he'd started to sprout hair and howl.

Verity regretted the fact that she'd picked up the heavier of the chairs and set it down. In as calm and even a voice as she could manage, she said, 'First of all, I'd like to say I'm very sorry about the misunderstanding in the car park.'

Now empty-handed, Verity took one very small step towards the man, contrary to the advice given by the part of her brain that governed self-preservation. 'So, why don't we—'

Donahue threw his arms up in defence. 'No! Don't let her touch me! She's going to murder me!' He took a step backwards, cowering behind his arms, which he held before him in the shape of a cross. Things were not going to plan, but in the absence of a better idea, Verity moved slowly toward him. This was clearly all too much for Donahue, who turned to the door and fled down the corridor toward the stairs.

No sooner was his back turned, than Verity ducked back into the office and slammed the door shut. She snatched up a chair and slid it under the door handle.

Donahue's footsteps could still be felt through the oak floorboards. His screaming continued unabated, 'Murderer! Murderer!'

Having sensed the coast was clear, Tony emerged from the footwell of his desk. He held aloft a fountain pen. 'There you are, you little devil,' he said, addressing the pen. He placed it on his desk, trying to avoid the scrutiny of the two women.

'Well, if I'm honest, Verity, I don't fancy your chances of getting this job,' said Leeanne.

Verity turned to Tony. 'What the hell was that about?'

'I have no idea.'

'Is he usually like this?' Verity asked. 'Because if he is, I'd like to withdraw my application immediately.'

'No. Never,' said Leeanne. 'He's a bit shouty sometimes, and he occasionally rubs people up the wrong way, but he's never gone completely doolally before.'

Her composure slowly returning, Verity turned to Tony. 'Perhaps you should go after him, and see if he's alright?'

'Yes, I should… I'll just go and check on him.' He approached the door with the enthusiasm of a man walking to the gallows and removed the chair from under the door handle. He placed it near the wall, and paused to consider the chair, as though he'd been brought in to Feng Shui the place.

Verity coughed, bringing Tony out of his stupor. He opened the door, and timidly popped his head out to survey the corridor. Emboldened by the distinct absence of Donahue, Tony exited the office and tiptoed along the hallway, toward the staircase.

Verity and Leeanne stood in contemplative silence. Verity was about to say she was going to leave, when Leeanne spoke:

'I think I should go and see if everything's all right. I won't be a minute.'

'Yes, okay. I'll just… stay here and sort this out,' Verity replied, instantly regretting it.

After Leeanne had left the office, Verity straightened up the office furniture and picked up the two fallen certificates and repositioned them back on the bookshelf. She wanted to leave—or part of her did, at least. That part of her—the sensible part—wanted to go home and forget all about the surreal events that had taken place in the last hour. However, part of her also wanted to know how things turned out, and that part almost always got its way. She sat down for a moment, fighting the urge to go and investigate, but she couldn't keep still. She went back over to the bookshelf and began to browse the titles. The books on display were mostly impenetrable tomes, coated in dust—chosen to impress, no doubt. In contrast, the bottom shelf consisted of a row of well-thumbed and dog-eared "Dummies" guides. Verity was looking out of the window which overlooked the car park when she heard a muffled cry from the floor directly above her. She looked up to the ceiling, her head tilted to one side, straining to hear what was going on up there. She heard glass breaking. An instant later, Carl Donahue shot past the window, headfirst. A scant second later, a dull thud reverberated around the car park, and Carl Donahue's journey into the afterlife was signalled by the sound of a two-tone car alarm.

4

DC Ulysses Hodge was a man of such hearty proportions he could be identified by his silhouette alone. He had fine, wavy brown hair, which was thinning on top, and a majestic yard-brush moustache, which completely obscured his top lip. Hodge considered himself to be the best detective in Brenton CID, which, given that he was currently the only experienced detective on active duty, did not say a great deal about his professional prowess but spoke volumes about his character. Hodge prided himself on his mental agility and his crime-solving statistics spoke for themselves. It was he who'd brought the infamous Hawbury Streaker to justice after tackling him to the ground in the middle of a crown green bowling match. And who did they turn to when they needed someone to bring the reign of terror of the Trewe Topiarist to an end? The very same DC Hodge.

Admittedly, a spate of more serious crimes had warranted bringing in detectives from neighbouring forces, but one man could only do so much, Hodge had reasoned. And as much as Hodge loved to bask in the glow of the media spotlight, it did sometimes prevent him from operating below the radar, where it was often easier to catch suspects with their guard down.

The detective felt sure that all he needed to take his career to the next level was to solve a high-profile case, and the death of a well-known member of the parish council, who'd met their Maker in unusual circumstances, fitted the bill perfectly.

By the time Hodge had arrived at the scene, they had cordoned the archway which led to the car park off with blue and white traffic cones. A fresh-faced constable greeted the detective and recorded his attendance in the scene log before briefing the detective about the incident. Two officers, one positioned at either doorway, prevented anyone from entering or leaving the courthouse. A third officer stood outside a rectangle of police tape. There were six cars inside the cordon. At the epicentre was an expensive-looking black Mercedes coupe with a sheet of blue tarpaulin draped over the front half of it, covering the mortal remains of Carl Donahue. The detective looked up at the broken third-floor window. Only part of the window frame remained attached to the stonework; the rest now lay in the gravel alongside the body that had displaced it.

Hodge stood a few feet from the police constable, his hands clasped behind his back. He rocked back and forth on his heels slightly and made pondering sounds for the benefit of the constable as he examined the scene.

'Nasty business,' the constable said, her eyes set on a fixed point in the distance.

'Yes,' replied Hodge. 'Murder often is.'

'Murder, you say?' She snapped her attention to the detective. 'I'd heard he'd gone a bit mad and jumped out of the window.'

Hodge had hoped his remark would get a reaction. In fact,

he wasn't sure this was a murder case. One would come his way, sure enough—it was simply a matter of when. But Hodge was not a patient man.

The detective tilted his head back and sniffed the air. 'Can you smell that?' he asked.

The constable turned to face the scene and took a few quick sniffs. 'Cheap aftershave, you mean?' She reddened when she identified the source of the fragrance.

'No,' Hodge replied curtly. 'It takes years of experience and a finely tuned nose to detect it, but the air is heavy with the stench of foul play.'

The constable wholeheartedly agreed the stench was pretty foul but was smart enough to keep her opinion to herself.

Without another word, Hodge made his way to the rear entrance, his hands still clasped behind his back. As he walked, the detective made a mental note to have words with the bloke in the pub who'd sworn on his mother's grave that the aftershave he'd sold him was from a warehouse clearance.

The moments that followed the incident were filled with chaos and confusion. Verity had heard someone running down the wooden staircase, shouting, 'Someone call 999. We need an ambulance, now!' By the time Verity had freed herself from her shock-induced stupor, she heard the same voice coming from the car park below. She'd tried to open the sash window, but it was stuck fast. She pressed herself against the cold glass, trying to see if what she'd thought she'd witnessed was real. With the glass misting up, and the difficult viewing angle, Verity could not see clearly, so she made her way down the stairs on unsteady legs. Two young women stood on the landing, hugging and crying. Downstairs, Verity saw Tony standing at the reception desk. He was on the phone, urging the call handler to send an ambulance as quickly as possible. The receptionist sat in her chair, sobbing and blowing her nose into a handful of toilet tissue. Leeanne stood nearby, her face buried in her hands. As Verity approached the fire exit, a man she assumed to be the caretaker stopped her. He put both hands on her shoulders and said, solemnly, 'He's gone, missus, and it's not something you want to see, I can promise you.'

Verity stepped back into the reception area and slumped into one of the leather armchairs.

An ambulance arrived barely ten minutes after the call had been placed, and the first of two police cars arrived a few moments later. The receptionist was standing near the fire exit, having a cigarette to calm her nerves, when she overheard one paramedic tell a police officer that 'life was extinct at this time'.

People wandered through reception in a state of shock. Many of them called their significant others to tell them what had happened. There were lots of "I don't know"s, "I can't believe it"s, and "I love you"s, and tears, and hugging, and an overwhelming sense of disbelief.

A silver-haired police sergeant arrived at the scene just as the ambulance was leaving. He took Tony to one side to speak to him and told him that a doctor would arrive shortly to officially pronounce death, and that someone from CID would be along to take statements from all of them, presently.

In anticipation of the arrival of a detective, Tony had gathered everyone together in the foyer. There were seven of them in all, and they had divided themselves between two green Chesterfield sofas and two matching armchairs.

Tony massaged his hands, trying to maintain the illusion of being in control. 'Now remember, none of us has done anything wrong. We just need to tell the police the truth, and we can get this… this terrible thing dealt with as quickly as possible.'

The caretaker peered over the top of his half-moon spectacles toward the door. 'Here's the old bill, now—or as near as we'll get to 'em, at least.'

The group turned their attention to the main entrance and watched as Hodge acknowledged the police officer. He pushed against the door with no joy. He pushed harder. Nothing. He peered through the glass and saw them all sitting there, staring at him. He tapped on the glass and mouthed, 'Open the door.'

'It's open,' said the caretaker through cupped hands, before covering his mouth and adding, 'you half-soaked sod.'

Hodge put his shoulder to the door and pushed again, to no avail.

'Pull it!' Tony shouted, miming the action as he did so.

Hodge flared his nostrils before he opened the door and walked in. The group found other things to occupy their attention as the detective approached them, in an effort to hide their bewilderment at the man's incompetence—if he couldn't manage a door, what hope did he have of solving a crime? Hodge positioned himself where he could see all of them and cleared his throat. 'Good afternoon. I'm sure many of you here all know me, and you know why I'm here, but, for the benefit of the new face amongst us,' he said, making a slow karate chop motion in Verity's direction, 'I'm DC Hodge from Brenton CID, and I'm here to investigate the death of a Mr Carl Donahue. I'm going to start by taking some details from you all, if you don't mind, before going over the events which led up to Donahue exiting the building via a third-floor window, along with your whereabouts at the time, so I can begin to recreate the events leading up to his demise. Now, before we begin, I'll remind you that none of you are under arrest, so you are free to leave at any time—'

'Well, in that case, I'm off,' said the caretaker, as he stood up and pulled a copy of the *Brenton Gazette* out of his coat pocket.

'Sit down,' the detective said. The man sighed and dropped back into the chair, shaking his head. 'However,' Hodge continued, 'if you do choose to leave, I will take your reluctance to cooperate very seriously indeed, and, given that the man who now lies dead, out there, on top of what was a very snazzy little Mercedes, was a friend of ours—'

Verity gave an involuntary groan.

'—I'm sure that won't be a problem for anyone, will it?' He turned to Verity. 'Are you alright? Is it all getting a bit much for you?'

'No, it's just that… the car... It doesn't matter.'

She had the detective's full attention now. 'No, please, carry on. If there's anything you want to get off your conscience, now's the time.'

'What?' Verity said, realising where the detective was going with this line of enquiry.

'It doesn't matter. Forget it.'

'But it does matter, Ms…?'

'Mrs Meadows, Verity Meadows.'

'It matters a great deal, Mrs Meadows. It certainly matters to the family and friends of poor Mr Donahue. It matters more than anything else to them. So, please, go on.'

Verity rested her head in her hands before speaking. 'The car he—the Mercedes—I think it's mine, that's all.' Verity wanted to disappear down the back of the chair.

'I see,' the detective said. 'You have my deepest sympathies for your loss, Mrs Meadows. However, unlike the newly widowed Mrs Donahue, I'm sure you'll be able to get a new one on the insurance.'

Verity closed her eyes and wished she were either somewhere else or someone else, right now—preferably both.

'Now, if you don't mind, I'd like to begin by taking down your details, starting from the person on my left.' As he spoke, he pulled a black notepad and a pen out of his coat pocket and flicked to a blank page. Pointing his pen at the man in the dustcoat, Hodge said, 'So, why don't you start by giving me your name and your particulars?'

The caretaker frowned at the question. 'You were married to my sister for four years, you know full bloody well who I am.'

'May I remind you that I am on duty, Brian, and I am here in an official capacity, and, as such, I will be addressed by my rank or simply, "sir". For as long as I'm involved in this case, procedures will be adhered to. Now, your name, please?'

Brian rolled his eyes. 'Brian.'

'Brian...?'

'This is bloody ridiculous. Brian Butterworth. Do you want me to spell that for you, or do you think you've got it?'

'No, I've got it, thank you. Now, continue.'

'I'm forty-eight years old. I work here part time, as the caretaker and handyman. I've lived in Hawbury all my life. I've got a dachshund called Colin, I'm a Pisces, and I like gardening, poetry and walks in the park. Satisfied?'

'I'll remind you that a man is lying dead out there. This is not the time for stupid comments and sarcasm. Understood?'

At this, the receptionist burst into tears. Tony put his arm around the woman and patted her shoulder. In turn, a woman to Tony's left began to cry, and he gave her a shoulder to cry on. Verity recognised her as one of the women she'd passed on the landing earlier.

'Well, you started it,' said Brian.

'So, what was your relationship with Mr Donahue like?'

Brian snarled at his former brother-in-law. 'You know—'

Hodge cut him off before Brian got up to full volume. 'Yes, I know what your relationship with Mr Donahue was like, but I'd like you to tell me in your own words.'

'Fine. I think it's fair to say we didn't see eye to eye on many things on a personal level because we'd once had romantic designs on the same woman, which led to a rather public falling out, but we kept that outside of work. When we were here, I'd stay out of his way, and he'd stay out of mine. That's all there is to say about it.'

'I see. And where were you at the time of the incident?'

'I was upstairs, in the CCTV room.'

'Doing what, exactly?'

'I was trying to find out why it's playing up.'

'Interesting. And where are the cameras located?'

'Let me see,' the caretaker said. He began counting off the cameras on his fingers, 'There are two covering the car park...'

Verity closed her eyes and cursed inwardly.

'One on the entrance to the car park; two in reception; one in the community room; one on the fire exit; one in all the offices, so that's another three; one in the staff room, and one on the landing of the top floor, which makes twelve in total.'

Hodge had turned away from the group and was looking up at the security cameras.

'And you say these cameras are "playing up"?'

'Yes. They have been for a while, to be honest.'

Verity dared to hope.

'Playing up how, exactly?'

'All sorts of problems: cables coming loose, water getting

in the connections, cameras just going off for no reason, and I've had to replace the main box of tricks twice.'

'I see. And are the cameras recording now?' the detective asked, waving a hand at one of them.

'Only the ones in the car park. I'm waiting on Naomi's dad to get back to me with a quote to put a new system in.'

Hodge was pacing up and down, running the top of the biro through his considerable moustache. He spun on his heels to face Brian. 'Convenient. Wouldn't you say?'

'Hardly. I've got better things to do with my time than getting up and down stepladders, fiddling with these ruddy cameras.'

Tony interjected. 'Steady on! How is this in any way convenient? Presumably, if the cameras were working, you'd realise that none of us had anything to do with this, and you'd see that this is just a tragic accident.'

The detective walked over to Tony and lowered his mouth to his ear. 'Yes. If it was an accident. But it's very convenient if it's murder.'

'Oh, murder, my arse!' Tony said, folding his arms defensively, and turning away from the detective.

'Touch a nerve, did I?'

Tony shook his head, too angry to speak.

The interviews continued in that fashion for the next hour. The remaining interviewees had the good sense to answer the questions as they were asked them, without questioning the detective's methods. It transpired that the two women that Verity had seen on the landing were Rachel Eaves and Naomi Wilson, both of whom held the position of assistant clerk. The older of the two, Rachel, who was still being consoled by Tony, had been in the main office, taking a call from a member of the public who was complaining about litter louts. Her relationship with Mr Donahue had been cordial enough, though he had tried to snog her at the Christmas party, until she'd kneed him in the groin. Satisfied that her claims could easily be checked, the detective moved on to Naomi. Naomi said that she was on the toilet at the time, as she had a bit of a "dicky tummy". Her relationship with the dead man was fine. When pressed, she conceded that she thought he was a bit of a sexist creep, but nothing more. Leeanne explained that she was on her way down to reception, following a brief exchange with Tony, having caught up with him in the hallway. Tony claimed he was on his way upstairs when he heard the window break. His relationship with Carl had been good. Tony had been Carl's best man at his wedding. He'd also loaned Carl ten thousand pounds last year, to allow Carl to finish some building work that had gone seriously over budget. In recent months, he'd needed to chase Carl for payment, but he was up to date, more or less, with the instalments. The detective noted all this down diligently, before moving on to the receptionist, and that's where things took an unexpected turn.

Hodge ran through the same questions he'd covered with the others. Mercifully, the woman's crying had subsided to low-level sobbing. Her name was Karina Nolan, and she'd been the receptionist here for the last eighteen months. She didn't really have much to do with Mr Donahue in the course of her duties as a receptionist, other than to put the occasional phone call through to him, and she'd sometimes see him if she took any mail up to the office. She also said she'd been on the phone at the time of the incident, which Hodge noted. 'But I don't know why you're speaking to me about this, it's her you want to speak to,' she said, pointing at Verity. 'She said she was going to kill him!'

There was a collective gasp. All eyes were on Verity now,

but none more than those of the detective. 'Did she now?' he said as he closed in on her.

Verity felt sick. Her vision began to distort, transforming the people around her into grotesque, hall-of-mirrors reflections.

'No. That's not what I said.' What had she said? She tried to recall the altercation with the man who now lay dead on top of her car. Her words came to her with alarming clarity. So much so, she could hear herself saying them.

I'll hunt you down and kill you.

'Okay. I did say that, but you've taken what I said completely out of context—'

The receptionist cut her off. 'No, I didn't. That's exactly what you said, I heard it loud and clear. I was standing no more than a few feet away from you when you said it!'

Karina's assertion had roused the detective. He addressed Verity's accuser, his pen hovering over a fresh line in his notebook. 'When was this and where were you when this happened?'

'Hang on a minute—' said Verity.

Hodge shut her down. 'No. You hang on a minute, and let this woman speak.'

'They were in the car park, they were. I'd heard a kerfuffle out there, and I thought it was those ruddy boy racers larking about, so I opened the fire door an inch or two and I could see her pointing her finger at Mr Donahue. "I'll kill you!" she said. Screaming, she was. Proper angry.'

Hodge made a note of this. 'And those were her exact words—*I'll kill you?*'

'That's right,' said Karina.

The detective turned to Verity, waiting for her response.

'No. That's not what I said, is it? What I actually said, if you cast your mind back, was "If you touch my car, I'll hunt you down and kill you." Which is a bit different from what you said, isn't it?'

'Wait a minute,' said Tony. 'Is that why Carl kept on calling you a murderer, just before he ran out of the office?'

'Did he now?' said the detective.

Things were going from bad to worse for Verity. If these were her jurors, she felt sure they would find her guilty on all counts.

'Hold on a second. First of all, what I said in the car park does not constitute a threat to kill. And as for him calling me a murderer, I have no idea what that was about, but I do know it's got nothing to do with me. For God's sake, I hadn't seen the man before in my life until a couple of hours ago.'

The detective was watching Verity closely, letting her feel the weight of the silence that fell between them, hoping that guilt would compel her to speak. He didn't have to wait long. 'There's no story here, detective. There are no skeletons in my closet, if that's what you're hoping for. I was just here for a job interview.'

'Go on,' Hodge said, observing her with such intensity that it made her feel distinctly uneasy.

'I arrived just before midday. The argument in the car park came about because he was driving like an idiot and very nearly crashed into my car as I turned in here. He started yelling at me, and I retaliated, putting him in his place. If what he said about the CCTV cameras is true, you'll be able to see for yourself.'

'Oh, don't worry, I will. Go on,' said Hodge.

'After that, I came straight in here for the interview, worried that I was cutting it a bit fine. But I needn't have worried as the interview was running late. Then Leeanne there made us a cup of tea while I waited, and after a few minutes Mr Henley arrived and we went through to his office to start the interview. We'd barely sat down when Mr Donahue burst in, ranting like a lunatic, screaming "murderer" at me before running out of the office. The other people in the office—Tony and Leeanne—went out to find out where he'd gone. After a moment or so, I hear a noise in the room above—a dull banging noise. The next thing I hear is glass breaking, then I see a man fly past the window, headfirst, and we all know what happens next.'

'Yes, we do. And I'm here to find out how it happened. In my experience, where there's a how there's often a who,' the detective said, smiling thinly.

5

Verity had tried to keep herself occupied in the hours following Carl's death. She'd been advised that a police officer would visit her that afternoon to take a formal statement. In anticipation of this, she'd tidied around the house, which didn't take long given that she was a tidy person by nature, and that most of their possessions were still in storage boxes. She'd tried calling her husband, Roger, to no avail, having done so half a dozen times on the way home without success. Her earlier text messages to him were still showing as unread.

The moment she fell idle, unwelcome thoughts over-whelmed her. Desperate to keep them at bay, she'd picked up a battered Marian Keyes novel she'd bought from a stall at one of the fundraising events in the village, and tried reading but found herself going over the same paragraph again and again, so she abandoned the book and turned on the television instead, only to turn it off moments later, after the third consecutive advertisement for a funeral plan.

Now she sat at the dining table, staring unblinkingly out of the window. After a time, it registered that her eyes were stinging, and she blinked a number of times in an effort to lubricate them.

On the table before her, a cup of tea sat untouched, now stone cold. A pair of reading glasses sat atop a neatly folded copy of yesterday's *Brenton Gazette*. The headline was a masterclass in alliteration: *Parish Peeper: Pervert Probed by Police*. They'd have a juicier headline tomorrow, Verity mused. She could see it now: *Local Man Dies in Window Plunge Horror* or *Councillor Dead in Mystery Fall. Outsider Quizzed by Cops.*

A police officer arrived later that afternoon. Verity was relieved to see that he was a regular beat bobby—a man in his early twenties, with a neatly trimmed beard and rosy cheeks. He was polite enough to take off his shoes before coming into the house, and he didn't take sugar in his tea, which was a good sign in her book, as she had a theory that there was a direct correlation between a person's intellect and the amount of sugar they took in drinks: The Whistling Plasterer, for example, took four sugars in his tea, whereas Verity only took one. It was an admittedly small dataset on which to build a hypothesis, but as far as Verity was concerned, this was a pretty reliable measure of a person.

She'd made a point of asking the officer to excuse the mess —of which there was none—and went on to point out the chocolate brown ceiling above their head. 'We've had to have a plasterer in to sort the ceiling—you might know him, tall man, whistles a lot.' She wasn't sure why she'd said this, but suspected that the officer might have encountered the plasterer in a professional capacity, for a breach of the peace or for assaulting someone's eardrums in a built-up area. The officer said he didn't know the man, which surprised Verity, given the plasterer's penchant for public disorder, but he assured her he would keep an ear out for him.

The process of taking a statement took about an hour and

a half. The constable had a pleasant manner, and he was patient with Verity, who needed to pause frequently to blow her nose or wipe her eyes. By the time she'd finished giving her statement, she'd managed to half fill a wastepaper basket with man-sized tissues. As the officer prepared to leave, he gave Verity a summary of what would happen next, telling her that someone from the CID would contact her if they had any further questions, and yes, it would probably be DC Hodge. At this, Verity muttered the word 'Great' in a sarcastic tone. The constable made no comment, but Verity sensed from his reaction that he understood her concern.

After the policeman left, Verity became very aware that she was alone with her thoughts again. She checked her phone. Still nothing from Roger. Rather than succumbing to the morbid memories from earlier in the day, Verity decided she needed to share her burden with a sympathetic ear.

Verity arrived at the local newsagents a few minutes shy of 6 p.m. She had walked into the village at an unusually brisk pace and was now quite breathless. She took hold of the well-worn brass door handle and held on to it grimly until her lightheadedness had passed. Once her breathing had returned to near-normal levels, she checked the opening hours. The sign on the door reminded Verity that Hawbury did not operate like the world she was used to.

McGee's General Store
Opening Hours:
Monday to Friday: 7-ish to 6-ish
Saturday: 8-ish to 1-ish
(Unless we're closed)

Sunday: Closed
(Unless we're open)

Verity tried the door and was relieved to discover that the shop was still open. A bell above the door announced her entrance. The shopkeeper appeared from behind an ancient wooden counter. The woman was short and plump, and looked to be in her seventies. She wore two moth-eaten cardigans, one green, one brown, beneath a tatty, blue and white checked tabard. Her hair was as bedraggled as her uniform, and was worn in a wonky beehive, the colour of seagull droppings.

On the counter before her stood a stack of unsold newspapers.

'What do you want?' she asked curtly.

Verity was more than capable of dealing with rude people, but she found that it helped if she had prepared herself beforehand, and this woman's display of rudeness had taken her quite by surprise.

At least most of shopkeepers in London had the good grace to barely notice you, she thought.

'Oh. Yes, hello. I was wondering if you could help me—'

The shopkeeper picked up a copy of the *Hawbury Clarion* and tore off the top section of the front page with several times more energy than was required, her face fixed in an uneven grimace.

Verity continued, 'I'm trying to find—'

The shopkeeper slapped the torn-off section of newspaper on top of a small pile to her right, hard enough to cause Verity to flinch. She then cast the remains of the newspaper into a large waste bin, which stood beside her.

Verity watched as the woman took the corner of the front page between calloused thumb and ink-stained forefinger.

'Go on,' the shopkeeper said sharply.

Verity cleared her throat before speaking. 'Yes. I was—'

Rip.

'—wondering if—'

Slap.

'—wondering if—'

The shopkeeper sighed and folded her arms, resting them atop her ample bosom.

'Well?'

Verity spoke quickly, determined to finish her sentence before this fearsome crone set about her.

'I'm looking for a woman—a young woman—'

'Aren't we all, love?' This comment flustered Verity, much to the shopkeeper's delight.

'What? No. What I mean is—'

'Are you buying or talking? 'Cos only one of them pays the milkman.'

Verity considered this for a few seconds. 'Yes. Of course.' She looked about her and her eyes settled on a row of confectionery, each item bearing an orange price sticker. Upon closer inspection, it was evident that the stickers had been placed over any promotional prices that were printed as part of the wrapper, and a price with a generous mark-up had been handwritten in biro on the sticker. Tourist tax, Verity thought. She was not a huge fan of cheap chocolate at the best of times, doubly so when it was being sold at inflated prices, but she picked two at random and placed them on the counter, being careful not to disturb the pile of torn newspaper.

The shopkeeper made a show of peering over the papers to inspect the goods. She gave a low whistle. Verity took the hint and added another two randomly selected chocolate bars. These had a message on the side: 'Part of a multipack. Not to be sold separately'.

She was not comfortable aiding and abetting this felon, but needs must. Verity placed the chocolate bars together and totted up the total price in her head. Two pounds and eighty pence.

'Is that it?'

'Yes, thank you,' Verity replied.

'Three pounds twenty.'

Verity was red hot at mental arithmetic and had to fight the urge to correct the old bat. She took out her debit card from her purse and looked around for the card machine.

'No cards under a tenner, or else there's a 50p charge.'

Verity bristled at this. This woman was practically La Cosa Nostra.

'Actually, it's now illegal to add a surcharge to card payments.'

'It's not a surcharge,' the old woman said defensively.

'Of course it is!'

'No, it's not.'

'Well, what is it, then?'

'It's a service charge.'

Verity couldn't believe what she was hearing. 'You call this service?'

The woman picked up the chocolate bars and dropped them into the large front pouch of her tabard.

'What are you doing? I was about to buy those,' said Verity.

'Not with that card, you weren't.' The woman glanced at her watch. 'Besides, we're closed.'

Verity knew this was almost certainly the only opportunity she'd have to get the information she wanted tonight. She looked about her, desperately trying to think of a way to win this woman's favour. She spotted a selection of dusty bottles of spirits on a shelf behind the shopkeeper.

'Wait. Give me two bottles of gin. I'll even pay the fifty

pence service charge,' she said, waving her payment card at the woman.

The proprietor made a show of considering it, before turning to take two bottles of some no-make mother's ruin off the shelf, and dusting their necks with the sleeve of her cardigan. She placed each bottle into a flimsy, semi-transparent plastic carrier bag.

'That'll be thirty-nine pounds and ten pence.'

Verity added extortion to the list of charges to be brought against the woman and moved her card toward the card machine again, but this time she stopped a foot short of it, before playing her gambit. 'I'm looking for a young woman called Leeanne—one word, not two. She's local. Works at the parish council. She's a bit...' Verity considered her words carefully. 'A bit of an eccentric dresser.'

The shopkeeper nodded. 'I might know her. And what is she to you? You're not from the papers, are you?' Verity considered the violence she'd just seen this woman perpetrate against the newspapers, and felt it necessary to make it clear she was in no way connected to the media.

'No. I met her earlier, at a job interview, actually, and I'd left some things behind, important papers and such—'

A look of realisation dawned upon the woman's face. 'Ah. So, it's you. You're the woman they're saying pushed Dirty Don off the roof.'

Verity felt her blood pressure shoot up. 'I beg your pardon?'

'Yes. Now I get it.'

'Get what? There's nothing to get. And what do you mean "pushed him off the roof"? It was a window, and I didn't push him!' Verity was furious, and it showed.

'Alright, keep your knickers on, sweetheart. I'm just saying what I heard, that's all.'

'Well, don't, alright? Or I'll have you up for slander.'

The shopkeeper showed Verity that her hands were empty. 'Fine. But it ain't just me saying it, everyone's talking about it. And what with him and his wife, and those poor kids. It's terrible, so it is.'

'Yes, it is terrible,' said Verity. 'But not as terrible as falsely accusing people of murder!'

The woman practically wilted under Verity's considerable glare.

Verity wanted to take advantage of this shift in power, and find out everything this insufferable harridan knew about the dead man, but the thought of spending any more time with her than absolutely necessary nauseated her.

Verity straightened and set her jaw. 'Now look. Just tell me where Leeanne lives, take my thirty-nine pounds and ten bloody pence, and I'll let you get back to polishing your broomstick.'

Verity was expecting the venomous old toad to give her both barrels, but she responded meekly. 'Fair enough. As it happens, I didn't much care for the man, myself, but if what people are saying is true...' Verity clenched her teeth hard enough that her jaw ached. 'And I'm not saying it is. Well, anyway. I don't suppose it matters what I think. It don't make him any less dead, does it?'

'No, it doesn't. Now, where does Leeanne live?' Verity demanded.

'She lives with her boyfriend. In the cottage opposite the old bank, just off the high street. Primrose Cottage, it is. You'll know it when you see it, that's for sure.'

'That wasn't so hard, was it? Now do you want my money or not?' Verity said, brandishing her debit card menacingly.

The woman rung up the amount on the till, and Verity put her card in the machine, half expecting the payment to be declined—an irrational throwback to that fateful evening in an undersea restaurant when her life first started to fall apart. Mercifully, payment was accepted, and she snatched up the bag which held her gin bottles and made for the door, yanking it open so hard that it almost separated the clapper from the bell.

As Verity marched victoriously out of the shop, the shop-keeper plucked one of the chocolate bars out of her tabard and examined its best-before date. It was fifteen months past its best. She frowned, shrugged her shoulders, tore open the wrapper, took a bite, and grimaced.

6

Primrose Cottage was instantly identifiable as Leeanne's home. Given the shopkeeper's snide tone when she'd given her directions, Verity had expected the house to resemble a miniature Las Vegas. Instead, she found herself in front of an oasis of colour in a comparatively barren landscape. The entirety of the front of the cottage was festooned with large, brightly coloured, metal butterflies. The front lawns were awash with an explosion of wildflower blooms. Garden planters in a variety of novelty designs—from Grecian urns to wellington boots—were dotted around the garden, each over-flowing with fragrant lavender. It was surprisingly tasteful, Verity thought, as she walked down the path to the front door. She pressed the doorbell and waited. Above her head, a wind chime tinkled gently, and a fat bumble bee buzzed by lazily. A man answered the door. Verity found herself smiling broadly.

The man was tall and dark-haired. He had a rugged complexion and the good looks of an aftershave model, though he was dressed in cargo trousers and a dark polo shirt, rather than cool white cotton. *Leeanne has done very well for herself*, Verity thought, as she shook herself from her reverie. The man eyed her with a noticeable degree of suspicion. 'Hello?'

'Hi,' Verity replied, still a little tipsy on the wonders of Mother Nature.

'Umm. Are you the police or are you here about Jesus?'

'You must be Gary. I'm Verity. I met Leeanne earlier, at the council offices. Is she in?'

Gary called out to Leeanne, 'There's someone at the door for you, love. She's not the police and I don't think she's a God-botherer—' He turned to Verity, looking slightly panic-stricken. 'You're not a God-botherer, are you?'

Verity smiled, 'No.'

'Thank God for that—no offence.' He turned and shouted down the hallway, 'Leeanne.' Leeanne appeared behind him. She was wearing a Scooby Doo onesie and was wrapping a towel around her hair. She saw Verity at the door and invited her in. Much like the garden, the inside of the cottage was not as Verity had imagined. The living room was tidy, but not fussily so. It was tastefully decorated in creams and natural oak. Splashes of colour came in the form of homemade cushion covers, vases of wildflowers, and framed pop art. There was a light sprinkling of their possessions throughout the room, but nothing in the room had been put there for show. This was the home of people who were at ease with who they were. Verity noted a sensation that she later identified as envy.

Leeanne took Verity's coat and handed it to Gary, who hung it up in the hallway. 'Take a seat,' Leeanne said. Before Verity could do so, Leeanne threw her arms around her and gave her a substantial hug. It wasn't a short hug, either.

'Sorry. I'm a bit of a hugger, aren't I, Gary?'

'She is,' Gary agreed. 'Can I get you a tea or are you

drinking your own?' he added, gesturing at Verity's bag. She looked down and saw the neck of a gin bottle poking through the top of the carrier bag. 'Oh, God. I look like a right lush, don't I?'

'Don't worry, your secret is safe with us,' he said, giving her a knowing wink.

Verity's cheeks coloured. 'Tea's fine, thanks. I'll take it as it comes.'

Gary went to the kitchen to prepare drinks as Verity sat down in an armchair, lowering the bag to the floor gently, trying not to draw further attention to it. Leeanne sat on a sofa opposite, tucking her legs beneath her. She leaned forward. 'How are you doing?'

'I don't know. Angry. Upset. Confused. All the above. How about you?'

'I'm all over the place, to be honest. It just doesn't seem real, does it?'

'No, it doesn't. Look, I hope you don't mind me dropping in on you like this, I just needed to talk to someone about it, someone who knows everyone who's caught up in this whole mess.'

'No, I don't mind at all,' said Leeanne. 'How did you know where I live? I don't remember telling you.'

Verity suddenly thought that coming here might have been a mistake. 'I was in the shop in the village—the one you mentioned earlier—and I asked in there if she knew where you lived. I hope you don't mind?'

Leeanne gave Verity a reassuring smile. 'No, it's fine, honestly. I'm glad you came.'

Gary returned with the drinks. He was carrying two mugs in one hand, and a generous glass of red wine in the other. He placed the drinks on the coffee table and sat down next to Leeanne.

Leeanne spoke. 'Oh, sorry, this is Gary, he's my boyfriend.' Gary rose from the sofa, extending his hand to Verity; she rose too, and the pair shook hands briefly. Leeanne continued, 'This is the lady I was telling you about earlier,' she said, giving Gary a subtle nod. Verity saw Gary's face change as he made the connection. She tensed, waiting for his reaction.

'Oh, yes!' Gary said. 'You're the one who went to that fancy restaurant under the sea!'

Not the response she had expected. Verity exhaled and felt her shoulders drop. For someone who was currently the chief suspect in a murder investigation, this was a most unexpected reaction. 'Yes, that's right.'

Gary regaled Verity with the story of the sharks and the underwater tunnels until Leeanne cut him off politely. 'I've already told her about that, love. Look, rather than sit here, listening to us two going on, why don't you make a start on dinner?'

'Alright, I can take a hint,' said Gary as he propelled himself out of the chair hard enough to cause his knees to pop. He picked up his mug and went to the kitchen, closing the door behind him. A few seconds later, pop music started playing in the kitchen.

Once she was satisfied that they wouldn't be disturbed, Leeanne turned to Verity.

'What is it you want to talk about?'

Verity realised she wasn't sure herself. She reached for her tea and gave this some thought before answering.

'I want to try to make sense of what's happened.'

Leeanne nodded. 'Me too.'

'And I'd like to find out a bit more about this Hodge character. He seems to have it in for me, for some reason, and I don't like it.'

Leeanne took a sip of wine. 'Don't you worry about Hodge.

He's not the brightest of buttons, but he's not the worst bobby we've ever had in the village, not by a long chalk.'

'Really?' said Verity, 'It's hard to imagine you could find someone worse.'

'Well, they did. My dad told me that when he was a boy, the village bobby killed his wife and cooked her up in a stew and ate her.'

'Oh my God, that's awful!'

'Isn't it just?' Leeanne said. 'Course, some of the old timers around the village reckon that's a load of old horse doings and said the pair of 'em moved to Margate when he retired, but I know which story I believe. Anyhow, I wouldn't worry yourself too much about Hodge, sweet, everyone round here knows him for what he is, and they pay no more attention to him than they have to. He means well, I'm sure, but this isn't the first time he's got himself all in a lather about a case, convinced that some so-and-so is guilty as sin, only for it to turn out that it was some other so-and-so that had done it.'

This wasn't exactly filling Verity with confidence.

Leeanne went on. 'Then there was the Hawbury Streaker, of course. Hodge still tries to dine out on that one, but it was hardly the crime of the century. The chap he caught was in his seventies, and he had a gammy leg, so he didn't take much chasing.'

'I don't see what any of this has to do with me,' said Verity.

'I think he just wants to make a name for himself by breaking a big case,' said Leeanne.

'Yes. And at my expense, it seems,' said Verity.

'Well, he's going to look pretty silly when it turns out that it was an accident,' said Leeanne.

'So, you don't think it was deliberate then?'

'By deliberate, do you mean did he jump or was he pushed?'

Verity hadn't considered the fact that he might have jumped. 'Pushed. I think if he'd intended on killing himself there are better ways of doing it.'

Leeanne agreed. 'And I don't think anyone would want to kill him. Not really.'

'What do you mean by "not really"? That sounds like you're not entirely sure.'

'I'm pretty sure.'

'But you're not certain?'

'Not a hundred percent, no.'

'What makes you say that?'

'Well, I suppose I *could* think of a few people who might want to kill him.'

Verity straightened in her chair, her eyes suddenly bright and fully focused on Leeanne.

'And were any of those people present when he died?'

'Oh, yes,' said Leeanne.

'Who?'

'Well, all of them, I suppose.'

Verity settled back into her chair, considering her next steps.

Seeing Verity lost in thought, Leeanne set down her glass of wine. 'Why, what are you thinking?'

'I'm thinking that I'm not sure that I want to leave my fate in the hands of Hodge.'

Cooking smells wafted through from the kitchen, reminding Verity that the couple would be eating their evening meal soon. She glanced at her watch.

'I don't suppose you could give me a list of the names and addresses of everyone who was there today, could you?'

7

Verity woke early the next morning, thanks to an unpleasant dream which had been more memory than nightmare. She had gone into the garden, wearing her husband's dressing gown, hoping that the morning light would drive away the ghosts. She sat at a bistro table at the bottom of the garden, staring at her mobile phone, watching as the signal occasionally rose to two bars, willing her husband to return her call. A disembodied voice called out nearby, startling Verity.

'Hello?'

Verity looked about her and saw no one.

'Hello,' she replied uncertainly.

The voice called out again. Verity stood up and walked toward the house. A head appeared over the top of her neighbour's freshly pruned conifer hedging. The head belonged to a gentleman of advanced years; a light brown Panama hat sat atop it.

'Major Reginald Ambrose at your service, madam,' he said, giving Verity a crisp salute.

'Hi. Verity. Pleased to meet you,' she said, raising her hand in greeting.

'Verity…?'

'Meadows.'

'Jolly good. Now, I'm sorry if I startled you, just then. I've been meaning to call on you, but you looked like you've had your hands full getting the old place spruced up.'

'That's the understatement of the year,' she said.

The Major looked about him surreptitiously. 'Besides, I didn't want to set tongues wagging, calling upon such a beautiful young lady, unannounced.' He lowered his voice to a whisper, 'Not with my reputation,' he added, a mischievous smile appearing beneath his immaculate, pencil-thin moustache.

Despite her current mood, Verity found herself chuckling.

'Tell me, is there a Mr Meadows on the scene at all?'

The mention of her husband's name caused Verity to glance down at her phone. 'Yes,' she said. 'He's working away, at the moment actually, overseeing a big property deal.'

The Major appeared suitably impressed. 'I say. Highflyer, is he?'

Verity looked down at her phone again. 'Well, I don't know if I'd go that far. He should be home in a few weeks or so, all being well.'

'Wonderful. I'll bet you're counting down the days, aren't you?'

'Yes, it will be nice to have him home.'

'How lovely.' The old man gave Verity a warm smile. 'Forty-three years, Jean and I were together,' he said, sighing wistfully. 'I miss the old girl, you know.'

Verity felt a pang of sadness. 'I'm sure you do,' she said, patting his forearm compassionately. 'I'm sorry for your loss.'

'Oh, no, she's not dead. No, she's taken up with that swine

from her aqua aerobics class. I should have known something was up. She couldn't stand being in water any deeper than her ankles, then all of a sudden, she's down at the local swimming baths more often than the lifeguard. They're currently living in sin not twenty yards from the church we exchanged our vows in. So much for "til death us do part". Anyway, to blazes with the pair of them, I say.'

She cursed inwardly at her faux pas. Verity had never been particularly religious—and any faith she did have had been severely tested by everything that had happened to them in the last year or so—but she believed that marriage still meant something. But who on God's green earth waited until they were knocking on for eighty to shack up with some new bit of stuff? If you were going to do it then do it while you still had some miles left on the clock.

She was considering how to make a strategic exit and save herself from further embarrassment when her phone rang.

The call was from a number she didn't recognise. Verity thumbed the answer button on her phone and held it to her ear. 'Hello?'

Silence.

'Hello. Can you hear me?'

No answer. She held the phone at arm's length and checked the signal strength.

'I'll leave you to it,' the Major whispered. Verity waved goodbye to her neighbour and headed back to the top of the garden.

'Hello, can you hear me?'

Finally, a voice at the other end of the phone. It was Roger.

'Hi. I can hear you. Can you hear me?'

'Yes, I can. I'm sorry, I think it's the signal at my end.' Verity returned to the table at the bottom of the garden and sat down, checking she still had a service. 'Whose phone are you using? I don't recognise the number.'

'It's a mate's. I've lost my bloody phone.'

'Oh. Well, that would explain why I didn't get a reply from you yesterday.'

'Yeah. Sorry, love. I lost it a couple of days ago. I should be able to sort out a replacement in a day or so. Anyway, I thought we'd agreed that I'd call you, and that you would only call if it was an emergency?'

'Yes, I know,' she said, struggling to think of a way of summarising recent events. 'Something happened yesterday, and, well…' She craned her neck, looking for any sign of the Major, before continuing, 'I suppose that it's an emergency of sorts.'

'Why, what's happened? You haven't smashed the car up or anything, have you?'

'No, I haven't done anything to the car, and I'm fine. Thanks for asking,' she said, feeling more than a little wounded. 'Well, that's not true. I'm not fine, but I've not been hurt or anything like that.'

Roger sounded relieved. 'Thank God for that. So, the car—and you—you're both—you're okay then?'

Verity took a second or two to compose herself. 'Yes, and no. The thing is, I went for a job interview yesterday—'

'What are you doing that for?'

'Will you listen, please?' she said.

'Sorry. Go on.'

'It was a disaster. It ended up with a man falling out of a window and landing on top of the car.'

She waited for his response.

'Hello,' she said, checking her signal again. Two bars.

Finally, he spoke. 'I'm sorry, am I missing something,

because it sounded like you just said that a man fell out of a window and landed on our car?'

'That's right,' said Verity. 'But that's not the worst of it. The police—'

'The police? Why are they involved—is he alright?'

'The man who fell onto the car, you mean?'

'Yes, the man who fell onto the bloody car. Who else would I be talking about?'

'No, he's dead.' Saying it out loud like that made it feel very real.

'He's dead?'

'Yes. And to make matters worse, the police seem to think I'm somehow to blame for the whole thing.'

'What? They think you killed him?'

She squeezed her eyelids shut in a vain effort to stop herself from crying. 'Yes.'

Roger let out a long sigh. It seemed that he was struggling to find words, too. Neither spoke for some time, though Verity could hear another voice in the background—a man's voice—only a word or two, though she was unable to make out what he had said. Roger spoke again. 'I've gotta go. I'll call you later.' Verity heard three beeps after the call ended. Despite this, she continued to hold the phone to her ear. Into the void, she whispered the words she had so desperately needed her husband to say: *I love you.*

Immediately after the call, Verity returned to her bedroom and fell face first onto the unmade bed, where she lay for almost an hour, feeling uncharacteristically sorry for herself. With each passing moment, any feeling of self-pity was steadily driven out by a simmering mix of resentment and anger. She was angry at Carl—or whoever was responsible for his death—for putting her in this situation. She was angry at Hodge for pegging her as his prime suspect. She was angry at Roger for cutting their call short, and not being here when she most needed him. But perhaps most of all, she was angry with herself for becoming a spectator at her own trial, which was being led by a bumbling village bobby. Verity knew well enough that, if managed correctly, anger could serve as an effective fuel, sufficient to light a fire under her and spur her into action. Logically, she knew that there was no case for her to answer, but her faith in the judicial system had been irrevocably damaged recently. She turned over and thought of the list of names Leeanne had given her the previous night. If she wanted the truth to prevail, she was going to have to go out there and find it for herself, then present it to Hodge in a gift-wrapped box. She threw herself out of bed and into the shower.

8

A short while later, with a need to visit a number of properties on the outskirts of Hawbury, and without access to a road-worthy motor vehicle, Verity had been forced to take drastic measures, and was now pedalling her seldom-used folding commuter cycle along unfamiliar country lanes. It hadn't taken much time in the saddle to remind her why she had abandoned the contraption in the first place—her legs were turning at a pace, but very little of the energy was being trans-lated into forward motion. She would be the first to admit that she wasn't great on a bike, but this thing must have been designed for use in a Victorian workhouse. It had three gears, and after several nervy gear changes which resulted in a terri-fying series of wobbles and weaves, it became apparent that one of them was neutral, and the other, reverse.

Verity had settled into her stride as she approached the main square. And while she was some way from being able to say she was enjoying the ride, she no longer felt she was one pedal stroke away from death.

After making a series of navigational errors and an

uncomfortable encounter with a cattle grid, Verity eventually arrived at Brian Butterworth's home, exhausted and bedraggled. She'd made the mistake of wearing a hi-vis walking jacket and now understood what it felt like to be a boil-in-the-bag meal.

Brian lived on the outskirts of the village, in one half of an attractive eighteenth-century farmhouse which sat behind a substantial dry-stone wall. Mustering the last of her energy, she opened the gate, wheeled the bike through, and propped it up against the wall. She collapsed onto a bench beneath one of the front windows and extricated herself from the jacket. After taking a moment to compose herself, she attempted to stand up, only for her jelly legs to give way beneath her. She was hoisting herself back onto the bench when Brian came around the corner of the house, pushing a wheelbarrow full of garden waste.

'If you're after them next door, they've gone into town. Won't be back til after two, I expect,' Brian said, as he forked the waste into a green waste bin. 'Wait a minute, you're her from yesterday, aren't you?'

'Yes, I am. Verity.' She extended a hand, but wasn't sure if she could stand up to greet him, so she turned it into a wave. He gave her a begrudging nod. 'So, what brings you here, then? You got business with next door?'

'No, I came here to speak to you, actually.'

Brian had finished emptying the wheelbarrow, but the garden fork remained gripped in both hands. 'Talk to me? And what is it you think we need to discuss, if you don't mind me asking?'

Verity eyed the garden fork and suddenly felt rather ill at ease. For all she knew, Brian was a cold-blooded murderer, and in her naivety, she might have delivered herself to the killer's lair. She had visions of being run through with the garden fork and dumped in the green bin. She thought back to the group interview and tried to recall the exchange between Brian and the detective, looking for something she could use to disarm Brian.

'Now I realise that this will sound silly, but I'm trying to work out why that detective has got it in for me.'

Brian narrowed his eyes a little. 'Hodge, you mean?'

'Yes, that's the one,' Verity replied, trying to sound more at ease than she felt.

At the mention of Hodge, Brian stabbed the fork into the small patch of front lawn and pulled off his gardening gloves. *At least there's a chance he'll leave DNA and fingerprints if he kills me*, Verity thought cheerlessly.

Brian dropped the gloves into the wheelbarrow and regarded Verity.

'I see. You do know that he was married to my sister, and not me, don't you?'

Verity laughed nervously. 'Very good.'

Brian remained unmoved. 'So…?'

Verity dropped all pretence and addressed Brian honestly. 'Look. I know this is an imposition, but this whole thing has got me in a right state, as you can imagine.'

'You're not the only one.'

'No, of course not, but it seems that your brother-in-law—'

'Former brother-in-law.'

'Former brother-in-law has singled me out, for some reason.'

Brian twisted an isolated patch of beard under his bottom lip for some time before breaking the silence. 'Fine, I suppose you'd better come in, then.'

Verity followed Brian around to the back of the house. He stopped at the back door to remove his wellingtons, which allowed Verity a moment to appreciate his bountiful vegetable patch.

'That's quite the harvest you've got there,' Verity said appreciatively. 'Is there anything you don't grow?'

'I don't grow any younger, that's for sure,' Brian said, rinsing his hands under the outdoor tap. 'Come in.'

The back door opened into a gloomy kitchen, which was dominated by a huge oak table. The table had been transformed into a DIY enthusiast's workbench, with most of the usable space covered with disembowelled gadgets, tools, spools of thin coloured cable, and a couple of CCTV cameras. Verity assumed that the cameras were from the parish council office, and this was homework.

'You'll be wanting a cup of tea, no doubt?' Brian asked.

'Only if you're making one.'

'Of course I'm ruddy making it, it doesn't come out the tap like that, you know,' he said.

Unusually, Verity was struggling to get a handle on Brian. She wasn't sure if his brusque manner was put on for effect or whether he genuinely didn't like people. As though sensing Verity's unease, Brian cracked a wry smile, and set about making their drink.

'Now, I only know how to make tea one way, and that's the proper way, using proper tea, made in a proper pot. If you want anything fancier than that, then I'm afraid you're out of luck.'

Verity had opened her mouth to speak, but Brian preempted her. 'And before you ask, the milk came out of a cow, and there's two types—with or without.'

Once he'd finished making their tea, Brian removed some of the electrical items from the table to make space and set a tea tray in their place. Then he cleared a stack of old gardening magazines off an old chair which stood next to the fireplace and dragged it to the table. He lowered himself into it gingerly, assessing the severity of the creaks and groans as the chair took his full weight. Once satisfied he wasn't about to end up in a heap, he poured tea into two stained mugs and slid one of them over to her. 'Help yourself to sugar.'

'Thanks.'

Brian picked up his mug and blew onto his drink with enough force to spray hot droplets of tea onto the back of Verity's hand, which she withdrew sharply. If Brian had noticed, he made no show of it. 'So, you're looking to get your head around our mutual friend, Hodge, you say?'

'Well, I'm trying to understand everything that went on yesterday, to be honest.'

'Aren't we all? A right flaming mess it is. And poor Carl... I mean, the bloke was a bit of a rogue, but he didn't deserve to clock out like that.'

Verity's mind conjured up an unwelcome Technicolor image of Donahue's body pressed deeply into the roof of her car. She shuddered. 'Who does?' she said.

'Oh, I'm sure I could think of a few people if I put my mind to it,' said Brian.

Verity's subconscious decided it wanted to play along and presented her with the unbidden image of one Marcus Pickering, complete with a tanned trollop and suitcase stuffed full of embezzled cash.

'Stop it!'

'I beg your pardon?'

'Oh, nothing. A sneeze, that's all. Hay fever, I expect.'

Brian pulled a face at this. 'Where were we? Oh yes, Carl. Like I say, he was a right 'un, he was.

'How so?'

'Eh?'

'You said he was "a right 'un"—a rogue. How so?'

'Oh, you know. Nothing serious for the most part. Got up a few people's noses, I suppose. Thought he was the big "I am", sometimes, liked the power that came with his position —like he was the ruddy Lord Mayor of London, or something.'

'I'm not sure that makes him a rogue, though?'

'Oh, no. That just made him an arsehole. It was his way with the fairer sex that made him a rogue.'

'Ah. So, you're saying he had an eye for the ladies—while he was married?'

'Carl's always had an eye for the ladies—usually other people's,' Brian said, his mood darkening.

Verity noted that the last statement carried some emotional significance for Brian and wondered if she wasn't beginning to make some progress.

'So, are you saying that Carl was having an affair?'

Brian didn't respond. Instead, he picked up a teaspoon and stirred his drink for the second time, seemingly lost in a memory.

Verity let him linger there for a moment and took a drink of her tea before repeating the question.

Brian removed the spoon from his drink and dropped it back into a crusty sugar bowl. 'I'm not saying he was having an affair. I'm saying he'd had affairs in the past.'

'And did his wife know about these affairs?'

'I don't know,' Brian said, testily. 'You'd have to ask her, wouldn't you?'

'Yes, of course,' Verity said, taking another sip of tea.

'What's that saying? "When a man marries his mistress, he creates a job vacancy".'

Verity nodded. 'I see.' *Interesting.*

'Who was it that said that?' said Brian. 'Oscar Wilde, I suppose, or Churchill.'

'Probably neither of them, though I'm sure the internet will tell you otherwise.'

Brian stood up suddenly, causing Verity to flinch. He picked up his drink and walked over to the kitchen window, which he opened before placing his drink on the side, and hoisted himself up to sit on the kitchen worktop. 'Anyway, I thought you'd come here to talk about Hodge?'

Brian's eagerness to steer the conversation away from Carl's extramarital affairs, and distance himself from Verity, was not lost on her. She made a note to take a different tack later, if the opportunity presented itself.

'Yes, well, as you saw for yourself, he just seems to have me down as his prime suspect—'

'And you're surprised by that?'

'What's that supposed to mean?'

'Exactly what I said. Are you surprised that Hodge thinks you're responsible?'

'Of course I'm surprised. Not least because there's no indication whatsoever that there even was a murder. And even if there was—which I doubt—I'd never set eyes on this Carl chap before in my life.'

Brian nodded. 'I know that, but that wasn't my question. I said are you surprised that *Hodge* thinks you did it?'

'Ah, I'm with you. Look, you don't need to spend much time in a room with the man to realise that he's as thick as two short planks, but—'

Brian shook his head. 'No, he's not thick.'

'Well, if he isn't thick then he's doing a pretty good impersonation of someone who is,' said Verity, crossing her arms across her chest.

'No, he's more… single-minded, would be a nicer way of putting it. Now don't get me wrong, I'm no fan of his, but to give him his due, he's like a dog with a bone once he gets an

A J FORD

idea in his head. He has to see it through to the bitter end, even though it'll lead him astray ninety-nine times out of a hundred. He'll get there, eventually—he always does. It's just a shame it's after everyone else has already crossed the finish line.'

'So, what you're saying is he's not thick, he's just… slow?'

'Correct.'

'So I shouldn't take this personally?'

'Hmm. I don't know if I'd go as far as to say that…'

'Great. This isn't making me feel better, you know.'

'No, I don't suppose it is, but you'll get the measure of him eventually—everybody does. Let's just hope for your sake it's from this side of a cell door.'

Verity recoiled at this needless dig. 'That's not very helpful.'

'Oh, get over yourself, woman. I'm only having a laugh with you,' Brian said, glancing up at the clock.

Verity took the hint and picked up her handbag from the table. 'Well, I'm not laughing. But I appreciate you taking the time to talk to me, all the same.'

'No bother at all,' Brian said as he opened the kitchen door for her.

'Thanks for the tea.'

'Thanks for the company. Makes a change from talking to the plants, though they usually make for more interesting conversation.'

Verity turned on her heels, ready to retaliate, to see Brian holding his hands up in mock surrender. 'I'm joking.'

Outside, Verity mounted up, but not before dropping her handbag twice, and putting on her walking jacket inside out.

Brian watched her struggle for a while before offering to throw her bike into the back of his truck and take her home. Pride got in the way of practicality, and Verity declined the offer. Brian watched her cycle away unsteadily before closing the door. He'd barely settled into his armchair when there was a knock at the front door. He opened it to find Verity standing there, looking rather sorry for herself, her jacket torn and flapping open at the elbow and a brace of bramble branches tangled in her hair. 'I don't suppose that offer of a lift still stands, does it?'

9

Verity sat on the edge of her sofa with a tea towel full of ice pressed to her grazed and swollen elbow. She had put the television on to distract herself from the pain, to no avail, so she turned off the television and sat back in the chair, careful not to catch her elbow. She thought back to her conversation with Brian, which hadn't been as illuminating as she'd hoped it would be, though she was relieved to learn that Hodge had a reputation for being a nuisance, as that was easier for her to deal with than a misguided personal vendetta. Her instincts told her that Brian was telling the truth about Carl and his serial infidelity, but she had a definite sense that Brian wasn't being particularly forthcoming when presented with an opportunity to say more about it. During the drive home, Brian had engaged her in some small talk—mostly about how she'd ended up in Hawbury—peppered here and there with some fact or other about whatever object of interest they happened to be driving past—the well, the butter cross, the corn exchange. It was all very pleasant, but something didn't feel quite right about it, so she decided to call the only person in the village she felt she could truly trust.

Verity deposited her cold compress into the kitchen sink and began waving her mobile phone around the room with her good arm. Once the phone settled at around two bars, she called Leeanne, who answered on the third ring.

'Hi, Leeanne, it's Verity.'

'Yes, I know. It says on my phone.'

'Right. Are you free to talk for a couple of minutes?'

'Yes, sure.'

'Good. Now—'

'When?'

'I'm sorry?'

'When do you want to talk?'

'Now, if you're free,' said Verity, bewildered.

'Yeah, I'm free. Go on.'

Verity shook her head in mild amusement. 'I've just been to see the caretaker chap, Brian, to get his take on things.'

'Okay. And did it help?' Leeanne asked.

'I think so—a little. But there was something he mentioned —about Carl having an affair—that I'd like to find out more about.'

Leeanne made the connection. 'I see. And you think that maybe one of his jealous ex-lovers or their other half might have killed him?'

'I don't know, but it seems like an obvious place to start, I suppose.'

'Well, that puts two people in the frame straight away.'

Verity sat upright. 'Really? Who?'

'Well, Brian for one.'

Verity's eyes widened. 'I didn't think he was that way inclined.'

Now it was Leeanne's turn to sound confused. 'What are you on about?'

'You know—Brian and Carl—being in a relationship,' said Verity.

'They're not in a relationship, you daft thing.'

'I was going to say. They'd make an unlikely couple,' Verity said.

'Don't most people?'

'Yes, I suppose they do. So, what's the story, and who's this other person you mentioned?'

'Hello? Are you there?' Leeanne said. 'You're breaking up.'

Verity glanced at her phone. One bar. 'Hello. Yes, I'm here. Can you hear me?' She'd have to get a landline installed, she thought, as she made her way into the back garden to get a better signal.

'Hello?' She was about to hang up when she a heard noise from Leeanne's end.

'You sound like you've fallen down the loo. Are you at home?' Leeanne said, pronouncing each word slowly and loudly.

'Yes, I am at home,' Verity said, responding in the same manner.

'Okay. I need to nip out to get some shopping. I can come round to yours first, if you like.'

Verity stood at the end of the garden. 'That's fine. I'll give you my address. Have you got a pen?'

'It's okay, I know where you live.'

'Really? I don't remember giving you my address.'

'You didn't,' said Leeanne.

'So how do you know where I live?'

'Everyone knows where you live.'

Of course they did. Jungle drums and wagging tongues. They'd have a blue plaque on her cottage before the end of the day, she thought ruefully.

Verity Meadows. Born 26.12.1971. Outsider, Road-rager, and Murder Suspect Lives Here.

Leeanne spoke, 'Are you still there?'

'Yes, I'm still here,' Verity replied. *But not for a moment longer than I need to be.*

'I'll see you in about twenty minutes, and I'll take you out for a cup of tea. Bye for now.'

'Okay. Bye,' Verity said, but Leeanne had already hung up.

The tearoom was not one Verity had visited before, but it shared many of the same features as the others; low beamed ceilings; whitewashed stone walls, dotted with period style wall lights; watercolour paintings depicting village life in a bygone age; dark wooden shelves lined with eclectic china and brass ornaments, and a revolving leaflet dispenser, half-populated with wilting and woefully outdated leaflets.

Leeanne took Verity by the hand and led her through a narrow archway to a vacant table for two in a quiet corner.

'This table's reserved,' Verity said, pointing at the sign in the middle of the table.

'Oh, ignore that,' Leeanne said. 'That's just there for the grockles.'

'The Grockles? Is this their table?'

'No. *Grockles,*'

Verity stared at her blankly.

'Tourists,' said Leeanne, loud enough to cause half a dozen unfamiliar faces to look up from their overpriced cream teas.

Acutely aware that she was suddenly the main focus of

73

attention, Verity sat down and shuffled her chair along until she was obscured from view by the separating wall.

'Embarrassing,' said Verity as she removed a sticky, laminated menu from its holder.

'So, what are you having then?' Leeanne asked.

'I'm not sure yet,' said Verity, extending the menu to arm's length, trying to get the text to come into focus. She sucked in air sharply through her teeth as pain shot out from her injured elbow.

'Are you okay?' Leeanne asked, a look of concern on her face.

Verity dropped the menu onto the table and nursed her elbow. 'It's nothing. I fell off my bike earlier and hit my elbow, that's all.'

'What did you go and do a daft thing like that for?'

'What, riding a bike or falling off it?'

'Both,' said Leeanne.

'Don't worry, I won't be doing it again. My career as a stunt cyclist is over.'

After a few moments, Leeanne called over a waitress and placed their order—tea and a fruit scone for Verity and her "usual". Verity summarised her conversation with Brian while they waited for their order to arrive.

The waitress returned and set Verity's order on the table before her, announcing each item as it touched the table, in a soft, drawn-out whisper, 'One tea... and... one scone.' Leeanne's "usual" turned out to be an aptly named rainbow smoothie, which comprised seven different fruits, poured in neat layers, and topped with a generous swirl of squirty cream and a chocolate flake. If ever a foodstuff had captured the essence of someone's personality, this was it.

'So, do you think he might have been *you know what* by one of his lovers?' asked Leeanne.

'I'm still not convinced that he was *you know what,* but if he was, that would be a likely motive. When we talked on the phone earlier, you said that would put two people in the frame straight away. So why Brian, and who's the other person?'

Leeanne used her chocolate flake to scoop cream into her mouth, then she leaned in and whispered, 'Because Brian and Carl were two angles in a love triangle.'

'Were they, indeed?' said Verity. 'And who was the third person?'

'Karina Nolan,' said Leeanne, leaving a suitable pause to allow Verity to digest this information.

'That's the lady who works on reception, isn't it?'

'That's her. Of course, she was Karina Miller back then,' said Leeanne.

'This was before she was married?'

'Yes. Must be getting on for five or six years ago now, I suppose.'

'And what was Brian's part in all this?'

'Well, he was seeing Karina in the first place. And it was all going rather nicely, by all accounts, until Carl turned her head with his fancy car and the promise of weekends away in his beach hut in Bognor Regis.'

'Brian was the injured party?'

Leeanne frowned. 'I don't think he hurt himself.'

'No, I mean… Brian was the one who got dumped.'

'That's right.'

'And you think that's sufficient motive for him to commit *you know what?'*

'It could be.'

'I'm not convinced that's enough of a motive—and why wait all these years? There's got to be more to it than that,' said Verity.

'There could well be.'

'Such as?'

'Karina.'

'What reason would Karina have for killing Carl? You said yourself this all happened years ago.'

'It did.'

'And?'

'Well, I don't like to tell tales, but she'd been spending an awful lot of time in Carl's office lately, and I reckon she was taking down a lot more than minutes, if you get my meaning. And by that I mean her knickers.'

'Yes, I got your meaning,' said Verity.

'And she had the brass neck to tell Hodge that she didn't have much to do with Carl. I wanted to say something at the time, but it didn't seem right.'

'But they're both married now, aren't they?' said Verity.

Leeanne huffed derisively. 'Since when has that stopped anyone?'

'True. But it didn't work out the first time and I'm pretty sure Karina said she was at her desk when it happened, so it can't have been her.'

'She might have used the back stairs, of course.'

'The back stairs?'

'Yes, it's supposed to be a fire escape, but Karina uses them because she says they're easier on her knees than the main stairs, and they're right behind her desk.'

'And they lead to the storeroom?'

'That's right.'

Verity took a bite of her scone and considered this. 'No. Carl was a sizeable chap. If he was pushed, then it stands to reason that it was a man who did it. And Brian has already admitted that he was only a short distance away when it happened. And there's no way Karina would know Carl was up there—and even if there was, she'd have to get up those stairs pretty quickly...'

'Unless they'd already arranged to meet up there?'

'But he was supposed to be in the interview, wasn't he?'

'That's a good point.'

'I think I'd like to speak to Karina and get her side of the story.'

Leeanne was out of her chair so quickly that it practically spun. 'I'll drive,' she said as she headed for the door.

10

At Verity's request, Leeanne parked her car around the corner from Karina's house.

'Are you sure you don't want me to come with you?' she asked.

'I think it's probably better if I go on my own. I don't want to turn up mob-handed and put her on her guard.'

'Fair enough. What are you going to say to her then?'

'I'm not sure. I'll figure it out as I go along.'

'How about "I've heard you and Donahue were bumpin' uglies again. So, spill the beans or we're going to the papers".'

'That would certainly provoke a reaction,' said Verity, as she got out of the car. 'Are you sure you don't mind waiting for me? I shouldn't be too long.'

'Of course not. Besides, I've got the new Dexter Fontaine to keep me company.'

'Who the hell is Dexter Fontaine when he's at home?'

Leeanne opened the glove box and pulled out a paperback. She held up the book for Verity to see. It was called *Two*

Damned Hot and had two muscular hunks in ill-fitting fire-fighters' outfits adorning the front cover.

'Dexter Fontaine,' said Leeanne, hugging the book, 'is a billionaire firefighter slash private investigator from Los Angeles, and he's got a huge—'

Verity held out a hand. 'No! That's quite enough, thank you!'

Leeanne looked crestfallen. 'I was only going to say, "mansion in Beverly Hills". Though now you mention it…'

Verity closed the car door and walked around the corner, her fingers in her ears.

The first thing Verity noticed about Karina's house was the sign on the gate which read, "BEWARE OF THE HUSBAND". The second thing she noticed was the husband. The third thing she noticed was his stony expression.

This would require a charm offensive, Verity decided as she approached the gate.

'Hello there, I'm—'

'You from the papers?' the man snapped.

'No.' *Why the hell does everyone think that?*

'Are you sure?'

'Yes. Very sure. Certain, in fact.'

'Well, you look like you're from the papers.'

It must be the Louis Vuitton coat, Verity thought. The journalists in this place evidently had exquisite fashion sense.

'I can assure you that I'm not from the papers,' she said, trying to maintain a smile despite this man's open hostility.

'Well, who the bloody hell are you then?' he asked, his demeanour shifting from stony to stormy.

Verity extended her hand in much the same way people do when they're about to stroke a dog they're unsure of.

The man on the other side of the gate responded by

folding his arms and clamping his hands in his armpits. 'I don't shake hands. I don't know where you've been.'

Verity lowered her hand.

'So, what's your name then?'

'Verity. I—'

'Verity what?'

'Meadows. I—'

'That's right. You're her from the wotsit yesterday, aren't you?'

What little remained of her smile fell away.

'Yes, I am. That's why I'm here. I was hoping to have a quick chat with your wife, Karina—she is your wife, isn't she?'

'Of course she's my wife! Whose wife did you think she was?'

'I mean, you're her husband, I assume?'

'Are you thick, woman? I've just said she's my missus, didn't I?'

Verity's shoulders dropped. She wanted nothing more than to get back into the car and for Leeanne to drop her off at the nearest distillery.

'Look, can we start again, please? I'm sorry that we've got off to a bad start, but if I could just speak to your wife for a few minutes—'

'About what?'

'About yesterday.'

He unfolded his arms and placed them on the top of the wooden gate.

'About what pacifically?' he asked, craning toward her.

Pacifically. Verity shuddered.

'About… Mr Donahue and—'

Nolan's hands tightened on the gate, hard enough to cause it to creak. She looked down at his hands and saw his knuckles blanch, then up to his face, which was contorted into a crimson knot.

'I can always come back another time, if now's not convenient,' Verity said, backing away slowly, not wanting to get covered in blood when the man's head exploded.

'How dare you mention his name round here!'

He opened the gate without taking his eyes off Verity and stepped out onto the pavement.

'I'm sorry, I didn't mean to upset you,' she said, turning and quickening her pace.

'Let me tell you something about Donahue, love. He deserved everything he got. I'm glad the bugger's dead!'

Verity was nearly at Leeanne's car now.

'I'm glad he's dead because it saved me a job!'

Verity tugged frantically at the passenger door handle. Nolan's ranting continued unabated.

'And if you come round here again, you'll be able to speak to him in person!'

Leeanne unlocked the door, and Verity threw herself into the passenger seat.

'Go!'

Leeanne pulled up outside Verity's house. Verity looked at her reflection in the vanity mirror. 'Look at the state of me. I look like Alice Cooper,' she said, running a tissue under her eyelids, wiping away tears and smudged mascara.

'I give up. I'm done.' She flicked the sun visor up.

'Done with what?' Leeanne asked.

'Done with running around trying to get strangers to confess to a murder that didn't happen. Done with this bloody place. Done with...' she paused, trying to ward off tears, 'trying to do this on my own.' The tears broke through her defences. Leeanne took her hand gently.

'You're not on your own. I'm here,' she said. The tears turned to sobbing. Verity squeezed Leeanne's hand tightly.

'Thank you.'

'Come here,' Leeanne said, wrapping her arms around Verity and pulling her into an awkward side hug. Verity wasn't usually a hugger, but she released her seatbelt and moved into the embrace. It was a wonderful hug—sincere and comforting, something she hadn't felt in a very long time, and this realisation made her cry all the more.

They sat like that for a few moments, not saying a word, until Verity patted Leeanne on the back, indicating that she was done. They sat up, Verity rotating her spine to work out a kink.

'God, I needed that. Thanks.'

'That's what friends are for,' said Leeanne.

Friends. She hadn't known Leeanne for long, but it dawned on her that, next to Roger, Leeanne was now the only person she could genuinely call her friend. Her so-called friends from "before" had dropped her like a hot potato the moment her money had disappeared. And now here was this woman, a relative stranger, someone who once wouldn't have appeared on the periphery of Verity's social circle, picking her up when she was down. Not because of any hidden agenda, but simply because that's what friends do.

'So, when's your husband back from this business thing he's on?'

'We can't say for sure. A couple of months yet.'

'Blimey, it must be important for him to be away that long while all this is going on. Is he usually away for this long?'

'No. This is the first time,' Verity replied, as she stared, unfocused, out of the passenger side window.

'What is it he does again?'

'Property development—overseas, mostly.'

'I'm surprised you didn't wait until he was back before you moved. I mean, it was hard enough when we moved into our house—and I had Gary to help me. Okay, he's not that bright, but he can carry a lot of stuff, and he's nice to look at, so it must have been really hard on your own.'

'It certainly wasn't easy,' said Verity, as she recalled just how awful that period of her life had been.

An easy silence fell between them.

'You don't think he's having an affair, do you?' said Leeanne.

Verity's head swivelled toward Leeanne, wondering where that remark came from.

'Gary?'

'No, Roger.'

'No!' said Verity.

'Sorry. I didn't mean anything by it. It's just that something very similar happened to me once. An old boyfriend, Lucas, his name was—still is, actually—he said he was working away for a bit, which was strange, thinking about it, because he owned the butcher's shop in the village. Anyway, it turned out he was giving the girl in the veg shop, across the way from him, an extra portion of sausage most nights. I got suspicious when he started eating his greens and coming home smelling of perfume, so I waited outside the back of her shop one evening and caught them at it on top of the Maris Pipers.'

'Oh, you poor thing.'

'Poor him, more like.'

'Why? What happened?'

'When he'd put himself away, he came running out of the back of the shop, begging for forgiveness, saying it would never happen again.'

'And what did you say to that?'

'I said she's welcome to your chipolata because I've always preferred saveloy, anyway. Then I kicked him in the spuds.'

Verity winced. 'And what about her?'

'Oh. She disappeared after that.'

Verity sat bolt upright. 'Disappeared?'

'As good as—she moved to Trewe.'

Verity relaxed. 'I see. And what about Lucas?'

'He's married now. Got four kids, which is surprising 'cos I kicked him really hard.'

'Well, that's not something I'm worried about with Roger.'

'That's good.'

'And if he was having an affair, I think I'd just set you on him,' said Verity with a smile. 'Anyway, I'd better let you get on with your shopping. Thanks for coming with me today, I really appreciate it.'

'Anytime. So, what are you going to do now?'

'I don't know. Get drunk. Listen to some Phil Collins, and generally feel sorry for myself.'

'I'd feel sorry for myself if I had to listen to Phil Collins,' said Leeanne. 'Why don't you come round to mine and we can get sloshed together. I've got a karaoke machine!'

Verity shook her head. 'I don't think so. I couldn't carry a tune in a bucket.'

'So what? Neither can I, but it doesn't matter. Gary will be at five-a-side tonight, and both my neighbours are as deaf as posts. Come on, it'll be a laugh!'

Verity considered this. 'Why not, eh? I'll need to put my face on and sort myself out.'

'That's fine, I'll wait.'

'What, you want to go now? It's a bit early, isn't it?'

'Yeah, why not? I'll do us something to eat first, to line our stomachs before we crack open the fizzy stuff.'

'I thought you had to go shopping today?'

'Yeah, I do. But we can do that on the way back to mine.'

'Why the hell not?' Verity said as she got out of the car. 'Give me ten minutes and I'll be with you.' She crouched to look in the side mirror. 'Better make that twenty minutes.'

'Okay.' Leeanne watched Verity walk up her garden path and wound down her window. 'Put one of your fancy blouses on—we always finish with 'Islands in The Stream', and you're being Dolly Parton, because I'm always Kenny Rogers.'

Roy's Megamarket was an independent supermarket on the outskirts of the village. It had originally been a cattle market and, based on the smell that was currently assaulting her nostrils, Verity was convinced that something from that period still lingered. Verity waited by the entrance as Leeanne went to fetch a shopping trolley. A young man—an employee of Roy's Megamarket—was using a pressure washer to remove graffiti from the side of the store. The daubing, which had been partially obliterated by the jet of pressurised water, teased the reader with "Warren Birch touches—". Verity tried to find an uplifting noun to finish the sentence but fell short. Based on the artist's choice of script, Verity assumed it was the work of the youth she'd seen scrubbing graffiti off the "Welcome to Hawbury" sign when she'd first arrived in the village. Above the main entrance, a vinyl sign displayed the store's slogan: MEGA CHOICES AT MEGA PRICES.

Once inside the store, the two women wandered through the aisles, with Leeanne working methodically through a shopping list on her phone.

'Can I help you get anything?' said Verity.

'You haven't shopped here before, have you?' said Leeanne.

'No. This is my first time.'

'I thought as much. You see, Roy's have a unique way of organising their shelves…'

Verity scanned the items strewn along the aisles on either side of her. 'This is organised? I thought there'd been an earthquake.'

'Apparently, they do it to keep you in here as long as possible. I know a woman who gave birth in the toilets here.'

'I'm sure that's happened before—women have given birth in some very unusual places over the years.'

'Yes, I know. But she wasn't pregnant when she came in here.' Leeanne snorted and nudged Verity with her elbow with enough force to almost send her toppling into a bargain bin full of puncture repair kits.

Despite her close call with the bargain bin, Verity couldn't help but laugh. She hadn't participated in such juvenile behaviour since junior school, and she was beginning to enjoy it.

'Oh, I tell you what you could get for me,' said Leeanne.

'A restraining order?' Verity replied, giving her friend a gentle shove to the shoulder, to which Leeanne overreacted spectacularly, practically throwing herself into a stack of toilet rolls. A security guard appeared at the end of the aisle and eyed them suspiciously. Seeing this, Verity straightened up and immediately stopped laughing. 'Sorry,' she said, as Leeanne picked herself up. 'She's started early this morning.' She mimed necking a bottle.

The security guard shook his head. 'You'd better pick them up,' he said, gesturing towards the scattered toilet rolls. 'And lay off the booze next time, Leeanne.'

Leeanne dusted herself off. 'Oh, get stuffed, Kevin.'

The security guard gave an exasperated huff and walked

off, leaving the two women giggling helplessly. Once they'd regained their composure, they continued shopping.

'You said you wanted me to get something for you. What was it?'

'Oh, yeah. Just some bacon and pork sausages, that's all. It'll save us both queuing.'

'Sure. Where are they?'

'They're on the butcher's counter, near the entrance. Can you get me eight slices of smoked bacon, eight pork sausages, and one chipolata sausage, please?'

Verity pulled a face. 'One chipolata?'

'Yes, just one.'

Verity stood in silence, waiting for the punchline.

'Honestly. It's for Gary—he loves them, but they give him terrible acid, so I mix it in with some vegetarian sausages for him.'

'Fair enough,' said Verity as she headed off toward the entrance.

'I'll come and join you over there in a bit,' said Leeanne, waiting before her friend was out of sight before grinning to herself.

The butcher's department was staffed by a lean, blond-haired man in his thirties. Despite his hairnet, hair protruded like straw from beneath his white hat. He stepped forward to greet Verity.

'Hi. Welcome to Roy's. What can I get for you today?' he said robotically, wiping a hand on his bloodied apron.

Verity surveyed the trays of meat, which were being closely patrolled by a squadron of flies.

She shuddered. 'Can I have eight slices of smoked bacon, eight pork sausages…'

'Any particular sausages, madam?' the butcher asked, as he deftly picked up eight slices of bacon and bagged them.

'Plain pork sausages, I suppose.'

'Certainly, madam.' He bagged the sausages with an unnecessary flourish.

'Anything else, madam?'

'Yes,' she said, looking up at him. 'Can I have one...'

It was then she noticed the badge pinned to his chest.

Her mouth fell open, allowing the words "chipolata sausage" to escape, her brain having issued the command prior to receiving a vital piece of new information.

Hi, I'm LUCAS. It's nice to meat you.

The muscles in his jaw bulged. Verity swallowed dryly.

He picked up the sausage links and held them at chest height. 'Just the one, is it, madam?' he asked through clenched teeth.

'Yes, please,' Verity replied.

'Are you sure, madam? We normally sell them in even numbers, you know.'

He picked up a pair of scissors with his other hand and held them horizontally, above the last sausage in the link.

'Yes, please, just the one,' said Verity, returning her attention to the selection of meats to avoid making eye contact with Lucas.

Snip.

The severed sausage dropped onto a thin sheet of white plastic on the counter.

She bloody set me up, the cow! Verity thought, feeling both embarrassed and amused.

Lucas bagged the sausage and placed it gently on top of the other bagged items, before looking beyond Verity and addressing someone behind her.

'Hello there, I haven't seen you in here for a while.'

Leeanne?

'Hello, hello, hello. Fancy seeing you in here.' The speaker was close enough to Verity that she could feel their breath on her ear. That unmistakable voice. The voice which spoke to her in nightmares.

Hodge.

'Do you mind?' Verity said, recoiling.

'Not at all,' Hodge replied.

Arrogant swine, thought Verity.

The remnants of Hodge's last meal were trapped in his voluminous moustache.

'Well, I do,' she said, swiping at her ear and inspecting her fingers for food crumbs. 'And what do you mean by "fancy seeing me here"? As far as I'm aware, it's still a free county—unless the Stasi have outlawed grocery shopping now?'

Hodge was unmoved by her comment.

'Precisely what I said. It's an amusing coincidence, that's all.'

'I don't think it's funny,' said Verity, considering the likelihood of this being a coincidence. 'You'd better bloody not be following me.'

'Paranoid, aren't we?'

'Given your recent behaviour, Detective, I don't think I am, no.'

Hodge stood with his hands behind his back. Verity noticed that he had no shopping trolley and pointed this out to him. Hodge responded by producing a shopping basket from behind his back. Verity's eyes widened visibly upon noting the basket's contents—three large tubs of whipping cream, a pack of hundreds & thousands, and a leather riding crop.

Seeing her reaction, Hodge glanced at the extended basket and withdrew it hastily.

'I'm making a trifle—for a friend, it's their birthday,' he said, loosening his tie.

'That'll take some whipping.'

'What's that supposed to mean?' he said.

'All that cream. There's an awful lot for one trifle. I hope your friend isn't lactose intolerant.'

'Stop playing games, Meadows. I'm getting rather intolerant myself—of your flippant remarks.'

'I'm just trying to give you some friendly advice, Detective.'

'Well, let me give you some friendly advice. Don't fox with me, miss, or you're liable to… get yourself into even more trouble.'

'"Don't fox with me" Did you really just say that? And what do you mean "even more trouble"?' she said, her voice loud enough that nearby shoppers lingered, keen to see how this played out. 'What trouble am I in at the moment?'

'You know what I'm talking about.'

Verity shook her head. 'Oh, you and your bloody "murder". Change the record, will you?'

Aware that a small crowd was gathering, Hodge lowered his voice. 'Murder is a very serious business, miss.'

'And so is proper police work. You should try it sometime!'

The two combatants had squared off, ready to go toe to toe. The assembled crowd now formed a loose semi-circle, which was broken up when Leeanne charged through them, using her shopping trolley as a battering ram.

'Get out of here, you. Go on!' Leeanne said, gesturing at Hodge as though she'd given him a red card. 'How many times do you need to be told? She's not interested, mate. She's happily married.'

Hodge stared, dumbfounded.

Sensing the crowd was with her—even some of the ones she'd just incapacitated—Leeanne began to get a little carried away with herself. 'And even if she wasn't married, she wouldn't be interested in you, would she?' She looked him up

DEATH COMES TO HAWBURY

and down. 'With your stupid sheriff's moustache and your stupid... old man shoes.'

Hodge looked down at his shoes—a pair of oxblood tasselled brogues—as he simultaneously covered his moustache with his hand, as though to protect it from these hurtful comments.

A man built like the entire front row of the Hawbury Hawks rugby team stepped out from the crowd. 'Everything alright here, ladies?' he asked, his eyes firmly fixed on the man with the preposterous moustache.

Leeanne spoke for Verity, who had retreated into a recess alongside the butcher's counter. 'It's him,' she said, stabbing a finger in the detective's direction. 'He won't leave my friend alone.'

'Is that so?' He rolled his neck from side to side. Hodge swallowed dryly.

'Steady on now,' said Hodge, frantically patting his pockets, looking for his warrant card, as the man closed on Hodge. 'I'm a police officer, and—'

'That's nice for you. Are you here to arrest anyone then, Dibble?'

'Not at the moment, no.'

'Then I think you'd better leave this woman alone, and be on your way, pal.'

Sensing that the mob was about to turn on him, Hodge backed away toward the main doors.

The stocky man suddenly lurched forward. Panic-stricken, Hodge turned to flee, knocking over a life-size cardboard cut-out of a police officer which stood by the main doors, bending the cardboard copper in half. By some miracle, Hodge kept his feet beneath him, and he stumbled through the automatic doors, which had opened just enough for him to pass through them. Security alarms began to ring. Confused and terrified,

Hodge turned to check on the progress of his pursuer as he ran into the car park, running directly into the open arms of the store security guard, who was only marginally smaller than the man Hodge was fleeing from. The security guard looked down at Hodge, immediately recognising him as the same person who'd started banging on the front door of his parents' house, gone midnight, some ten years ago, on the pretence of breaking up a clandestine school leavers' party. The copper, who had clearly had more to drink than many of the youths at the party, flashed his warrant card and demanded that they put all their unopened bottles into a large carrier bag that the officer happened to have in his possession, before staggering down the hallway and out into the night, singing 'Football's Coming Home', badly.

Kevin tapped the shopping basket in Hodge's hand and grinned. 'Have you got a receipt for these items, mate?'

11

Verity was woken by the sound of distant singing. She peeled open a gummy eyelid and rolled a bloodshot eye around to survey her surroundings. Not her bedroom. Weighed down by fatigue, her eyelid closed again. Her hands explored her surroundings. Not her bed. Somewhere, the singing persisted.

'We rely on each other, ah ha.

'Cause we love one another, ah ha.'

Sleep clawed at Verity, keen to pull her down into its murky depths, and she welcomed its embrace…

Nearby, a toilet flushed.

Verity opened her eyes and tried to sit up. Bad idea. She fell back against the sofa and braced herself as a wave of nausea washed over her. 'Oh God,' she moaned, as she ran internal diagnostics, trying to determine what was wrong with her.

'Islands in the stream,

That is what we are.'

Fragments of memories from the previous night returned. A disco ball. Song lyrics on the TV. Standing on a table. *Drinks on fire?* Falling off a table. Laughing. Hugging. Crying. *A concrete wellington?*

'No. You didn't, you didn't,' she murmured. She opened her eyes again and manoeuvred herself into a semi-sitting position, trying to fill in the blanks in her memory.

Did you?

In an attempt to reposition herself on the sofa, Verity placed one hand on the floor and found a plastic bowl, which was mercifully empty—unlike the concrete wellington.

You did.

'Morning!' Leeanne said, as she threw open the living room curtains. Verity recoiled from the sunlight. 'How's your head?'

Verity tried to find words, but the best she could manage was a throaty, 'Ugh.'

'Yes, I thought you might be. You were on a mission last night.'

'Oh, my brain hurts,' said Verity, her head in her hands.

'I'm not surprised. You were knocking drinks back like a Russian sailor. Everything from sambuca to sherry. I tried to get you to slow down, but you weren't having it. We had a good laugh though, didn't we?'

Verity threw back the duvet and stood up, taking a few seconds for the room to become still. 'Toilet,' she said in a hoarse whisper, her vocal cords shredded by singing and vomiting.

'Straight through that door there and it's right in front of you,' said Leeanne, pointing at the kitchen door.

Verity sat on the toilet with her heavy head over the adjacent sink. Part of her wanted to die, but she worried that death might be an eternity of feeling like this. Something odd was going on with her chest. She looked down to discover one of her breasts had swollen dramatically. Under normal circumstances, she would have panicked. Instead, she fumbled at the buttons on her blouse, and opened it. Reaching inside, she pulled out a withered blue balloon.

When Verity was sure she wasn't going to throw up again, she stood at the sink and washed her hands. When she looked in the mirror she gave a start, ready to fight off the woman with the big bleached-blonde hair. She turned back to the mirror and placed her hands on her head, exploring the nylon curls.

You can be Dolly Parton...

Verity shuffled out of the bathroom and over to the sofa and lowered herself down carefully, trying not to make her already thunderous headache any worse.

'Tea?' Leeanne asked brightly, as she moved around the living room, picking up an embarrassing number of empty bottles from the table.

'Please. Have you got any headache tablets?' asked Verity.

'I'll get you some.'

'Thanks.'

'I'm doing breakfast in a bit. Do you want some?'

The thought of food caused Verity's stomach to lurch.

'God, no.'

'Are you sure? It'll do you the power of good? I swear by a big fry-up after—'

Verity shook her head gently. 'Please, stop.'

'That bad, eh?'

'Hmm, hmm.'

'How about a hangover smoothie instead?'

Verity whimpered.

'Tea it is then,' Leeanne said as she went into the kitchen. Verity took off the blonde wig and rubbed her aching scalp.

Leeanne served the tea outside, despite the fact that rain had been forecast for that morning, reasoning that the fresh air would do Verity good—and if it didn't, she was only a short distance from an empty concrete planter.

Verity took two proffered paracetamol and washed them down with a large glass of water before sipping her tea, its warmth soothing her throat. 'I'm so sorry if I embarrassed myself last night; I haven't drunk like that since I was a teenager.'

'Don't be daft, you didn't embarrass yourself much at all.'

Much.

'Oh God, what did I do? No, better still, don't tell me. I don't want to know.'

Leeanne pulled her phone out of the pocket of her Dalmatian-dappled dressing gown. 'I've got some videos if you want to see them.'

Video evidence is admissible in court, Verity thought. 'No, thank you. I'd rather watch my own execution.'

'Are you sure? There are some pretty funny ones.'

Despite her sense of foreboding, curiosity got the better of her. 'Go on then, but promise me you'll delete them if they're as bad as I think they're going to be.'

'Oh,' Leeanne said, meekly. 'Do you want me to delete them from my phone and the internet?'

Verity's shoulders dropped. 'Please say you didn't put them on the internet.

'Okay. I'll say that if it helps.'

Verity massaged her temples. 'Dear God, kill me now.'

The silence was only broken when Leeanne slurped her tea, causing Verity to massage her temples all the harder.

'I'm only messing with you! They're not on the internet!'

Verity took her head out of her hands and breathed a sigh of relief. 'Oh, thank God for that!'

'They're not that bad, anyway. Here, watch this.' Leeanne

held her phone in front of the both of them and pressed play. The video showed them in the middle of the living room, beneath a spinning disco ball, singing along to 'The Time Warp'. Verity was squinting at the TV screen, valiantly attempting to sing the right lyrics at the right time, in contrast to Leeanne, who was belting out the song without needing to consult the screen. Now they were dancing—Leeanne executing the pelvic thrust perfectly, while Verity's moves more closely resembled something between the Macarena and the Charleston.

'Who took this video?' Verity asked.

'We always set up a camera, so we can watch ourselves the next day. It's more fun that way.'

Hungover Verity wasn't at all convinced this was fun, but Drunk Verity was clearly having a great time, despite her obvious inability to sing or dance. As cringeworthy as her performance was, it was fascinating to watch herself let go of her inhibitions and be completely consumed by the moment. Logically, Verity knew it was her on the screen, but it felt like she was watching another version of herself—her old self, a young, confident, happy Verity.

God, I miss her.

The video ended, and Leeanne looked up from her phone, still smiling.

'See,' she said. 'You didn't embarrass yourself that much, did you?'

Leeanne put her phone in her pocket. 'So, are you sure I can't tempt you with breakfast?'

The prospect of even seeing a fry-up turned her stomach. 'No, thank you. I'm sorry, but I just can't face it.'

'Okay. No problem.'

'Actually, I think I'd just like to go home and crawl into my pit and die.'

Leeanne gave her a sympathetic look. 'If you give me a few minutes to get dressed, I'll take you home.'

'It's fine, honestly, I'll walk. The fresh air will do me good, anyway.' It was bad enough that she'd vomited in her friend's garden, she couldn't risk doing the same in her car; Verity valued their friendship too much.

Leeanne subjected Verity to a hug. 'Okay then.'

'Ooof! Don't squeeze me, for God's sake.'

Leeanne released Verity and escorted her to the door. 'I'll give you a call later, to make sure you're alright,' she said, and watched her friend weave her way down the garden path.

Once Verity was some distance away, Leeanne shut the front door, took out her phone, logged into her social media accounts, and frantically started deleting bad karaoke videos.

The distance between the two houses was just over a mile, a journey Verity would usually complete in about fifteen minutes. This morning it took her twice as long. She was flagging now, but the sight of her cottage and the prospect of sleep spurred her on. She had just reached her gate when the Major appeared at his, watering can in hand.

'Beautiful morning, isn't it?'

Verity hadn't noticed. 'Is it?'

She propped herself up with one arm on the gate and lifted the latch with the other. The gate flew open, and Verity disappeared from view.

Verity looked skyward, squinting against the unwelcome brightness. The Major's face appeared above her, eclipsing the sun.

'Rough night, was it?'

Verity nodded gingerly.

She woke to the sound of a petrol lawn mower starting up outside her bedroom window. She sat up and drained the last of the water from a bottle beside her bed, pleased to note that the worst of her headache had subsided. She'd slept in her clothes but had at least managed to remove her bra before falling into bed. She went to the bedroom window and looked down to see her neighbour pushing a lawnmower, the beginnings of a neat stripe appearing as he walked toward the cottage. Sensing movement at the window, the Major looked up and raised his hat to her.

Verity wasn't sure how she felt about this. They'd had a gardener for years, back in London, but that had been a professional arrangement. She wasn't comfortable with someone taking it upon themselves like this. How much should one pay a neighbour to mow the lawn? She had to offer him something, but didn't want to offend him. She considered this as she put her bra back on and made her way downstairs.

'Ah, good afternoon. Back in the land of the living, I see.'

Was it afternoon already?

Verity responded, but he couldn't hear her over the noise of the lawnmower engine. He killed the engine and cupped a hand to his ear.

'I said, I've been meaning to do this myself, but I haven't got round to buying a lawnmower yet.'

'What's that?'

'Doesn't matter!' she said and went back inside.

Verity closed the kitchen curtains and sat down. It was bad enough that she was letting an octogenarian cut her grass; she couldn't watch him do it as well.

Verity heard the lawnmower engine cut off, followed shortly by a knock on the back door.

She got up to answer it, but the Major was already over the threshold. 'Hello?'

Verity entered the kitchen.

'Ah, hello there. How's the head?'

'Better now, thank you,' said Verity, still exquisitely embarrassed that she'd allowed herself to get into such a state.

'Good-oh.'

There was a brief silence.

'Anyway, I'm all done.'

Verity read between the lines.

'Oh, sorry. Let me just go and grab my purse,' she said, indicating that it was upstairs. She returned a moment later, purse in hand. Now for the awkward moment of negotiating a fair price.

She opened the clasp on her purse and flicked through the banknotes, all the time trying to determine a fair price for the man's toil. She had no idea what they'd paid their previous gardener, as Roger had always taken care of that. If only he were here now, she thought. He'd have taken care of the lawn, or at least negotiated a price for the job beforehand.

'Will ten pounds cover it?'

'I beg your pardon?'

Subtle.

Verity looked in her purse again. Damn. No fivers. It would have to be twenty pounds, as she couldn't ask him for change. She extracted a twenty-pound note and held it out to him.

The Major gave her a puzzled look. He looked at the money in her hand.

'What are you doing?' the Major asked, turning his good ear toward her.

'Paying you.'

'Paying me?'

'Yes. For the lawn.'

Finally, he understood. 'Over my dead body!' he said, waving the money away.

'I'm sorry, I didn't mean to offend you,' she said, putting the money back in her purse.

Verity scrambled to think of a way to smooth things over. *Tea*, she thought. *Old people cannot resist a cup of tea.*

As Verity had hoped, the offer of a cup of tea made things better, and they'd soon moved on from the embarrassing incident. While Verity was brewing up, the Major popped back home and returned with a small coffee and walnut cake, which was missing a slice. Verity still didn't feel up to eating but was mindful that she didn't want to offend her neighbour for the second time in as many minutes. It was a good cake, certainly better than anything she could produce. She asked the Major where he'd bought it from and was surprised to learn that he'd baked it himself. It was Marjorie's recipe. She'd left him with three things, he said: happy memories, a cake recipe, and an anti-social ginger tom called Peanuts.

They'd chatted pleasantly over their tea and shared a few laughs. Now that they'd finished, the Major's tone became more serious.

'Now, I'd like to propose something, Meadows, and I won't take no for an answer.'

'Okay,' Verity said, cautiously. 'As long as it isn't marriage.'

'Good God, no! No offence,' he replied. 'I've had quite enough of that nonsense for one lifetime, thank you!'

Verity breathed again.

'Now, I hear you're in a bit of a jam on the transportation front, and I think I've got a solution that will benefit of us both.'

'I'm listening.'

He asked Verity to follow him to his house. There, he

pulled open the garage door to reveal what she assumed was a car under a cream-coloured canvas cover. It was an unusual shape, whatever it was.

With Verity's help, the Major removed the cover from the car, to reveal a pristine grey Morris 1000 Traveller, with red leather seats, and what appeared to be a wooden steering wheel. There was even wood on the outside of the car. Actual wood.

'Isn't she a beauty?' he said, admiring the car as though it were a thing of flesh and blood.

Verity struggled to find the words.

He patted the roof gently. 'They don't make them like they used to, that's for sure,' he said.

'No, they don't,' she said. 'And with very good reason, I suspect.'

12

Leeanne sat on her front doorstep, humming quietly to herself as she waited for Verity to collect her. She was wearing dungarees, yellow Dr Martens boots, and a rainbow-striped sweater. Gary had said the outfit made her look like a children's TV presenter, to which Leeanne replied it was time that Gary stopped watching children's television.

Verity had called her a short time ago, saying she needed help with something, and Leeanne was more than happy to agree, as it meant she didn't have to visit Gary's mother with him.

The sound of an old car approaching got Leeanne's attention.

That looks like the car the midwife drives in that olden times TV show, Leeanne thought, as the Morris Traveller drew nearer. She was surprised when it stopped outside her gate, and even more surprised when she saw who was driving it.

Verity took a moment to work out how to open the window, when she saw the silver winding handle. *God, the indignity.* It must have been a quarter of a century since she'd used a handle to open a car window. Verity beckoned Leeanne over. 'Get in, and don't say a word!'

Leeanne approached the car, wondering if she was dreaming. 'Umm. Have you mugged a pensioner and hot-wired their car, or have we gone back in time?'

'Not a word!'

Leeanne went around to the passenger side of the car and got in.

'How do I close the door?' she asked, when faced with the absence of an internal door handle.

'That leather strap, there,' said Verity, pointing it out to her. 'Grab it and pull it.'

After a series of checks and a crunch of gears, Verity pulled away. Leeanne looked around the car, marvelling at its interior. It had a combination of smells like nothing she'd experienced before—oil and warm metal... mildew... wood and leather, and... old age. She touched everything within reach, taking time to register their contrasting textures. 'I love it,' she said, grinning at Verity. 'How come you're driving this?'

'Don't get used to it, it's not mine,' said Verity, clearly not sharing her friend's love of the car. 'It's the old chap's from next door. He's given me the use of it until I get my own car sorted out.'

'Oh, right. Mr Ambrose. That's good of him.'

'Yes,' said Verity. 'I just need to run him around from time to time, to doctors' appointments, and what have you.'

'Bless him. So, what's happening with your car then?'

Verity was focused on driving, as they bounced down the narrow lane that connected their two properties.

'There's some mix up with the insurance and I'm trying to find the paperwork, but it must still be in storage,' said Verity, stamping on the brake as a car entered the road ahead from a side lane. The vintage car's deceleration was not commensurate with the amount of force Verity had applied to the pedal, and they came perilously close to the car in front. The driver in front was oblivious to the fact that they'd nearly caused a crash, and they pulled away effortlessly. Leeanne crossed herself silently. 'We can take my car next time, you know. I don't mind.'

———

'Ooh, this is nice,' said Leeanne, as she stepped into her friend's home for the first time. 'I like what you've done with it.'

'I'm not sure I've done that much to it, other than to stop it leaking when it rains, and slap on some fresh paint. Most of my things are still packed away, as you'll see in a minute.'

After making drinks, Verity took Leeanne upstairs and shouldered open the door to the study.

'Excuse the chaos. I'm still living out of cardboard boxes.'

As forewarned, the study was divided into two distinct zones: chaos and order. Chaos took the form of labelled cardboard boxes, bin bags, and suitcases. The orderly half of the room contained a desk, which held a laptop, table lamp and a printer, two plush leather office chairs, and a corner shelf, on which stood a matching set of green leather-bound novels.

Leeanne picked up one of the books. *Murder In the Mirror* by Constance Beaumont, it said in embossed gold text. She flicked through it and sniffed the pages. It looked old, but it didn't have the musty smell she associated with old books. 'Is this one of those books you said you publish?'

Verity placed two coasters onto the desk and placed her drink down. 'Yes,' she said, taking the book and placing it carefully back on the shelf.

'How come it looks old, but it's not?'

'Because they're new. They were never published during my grandmother's lifetime because she didn't think anyone would want to read them, so when I inherited the manuscripts, I had this set handmade.'

Leeanne took a closer look at the spines of the books and saw a silhouette of a woman's head.

'Is that your granny?'

'Yes.'

'That's lovely. Are they any good?'

'I think they're terrific.'

'Do you sell many of them?'

'Not a huge amount, but just knowing that her books are out there is enough for me. Anyway, moving on, this is what I need your help with,' she said, turning her attention to the wall behind the desk. Three large whiteboards, raised up on large plastic storage containers, were propped up against the wall. Only the middle board had anything on it—a rough drawing of three floor plans. Leeanne inspected it, recognising it immediately as the council offices. Some of the rooms had circles with two letters in them: CD, KN, BB, LK, and so on—initials of the people who were present when Mr Donahue died.

'I get it. This is like Cluedo, but real life.'

'Yes, I suppose it is. But unfortunately, in this version, Hodge's envelope contains the cards: Verity Meadows, in the Storage Room, with the Hefty Shove, and I intend to prove that's not the case.'

'But I thought you said you were done with all this investigating?'

'I was, but that was before I bumped into the defective constable in the supermarket. If he wasn't out to get me before, he is now. And given my recent experiences, I'm not sure I can count on the legal system doing the right thing.'

'That's understandable, after what you and Roger have been through,' said Leeanne, as she wheeled her chair closer to the whiteboards. 'So, what's the plan, and what do you need me to do?'

'Okay!' Verity said with a clap as she stood up. She picked up a red marker and wrote the word SUSPECTS on the right-hand board. Immediately below this, she listed the names of all those present, excluding herself and Leeanne.

'Hang on,' Leeanne said. 'Why aren't our names on there, too?'

'Because I know I didn't murder anyone,' said Verity.

'And what about me?' said Leeanne. 'How do you know I didn't do it?'

'That's a very good question,' said Verity as she placed both hands on the armrests of Leeanne's chair and moved her face within inches of hers.

'Did you murder Carl Donahue?'

'No, of course I didn't murder him! We don't even know he was murdered, remember?'

'Good,' Verity said as she returned to the board.

'Is that it?' Leeanne asked, looking as though she'd been short-changed. 'A "Did you do it?", and that's it?'

'For you, yes, but not this lot,' Verity said, tapping the board with the marker.

At that same moment, in a stuffy, windowless room deep within Brenton police station, detectives Hodge and Yates stood before a whiteboard, considering the potential murder suspects.

For as long as she could remember, Olivia Yates had dreamt of becoming a police officer. After completing an MA in Criminology and Criminal Justice, Yates had followed in her father's footsteps and joined Brenton Police Service. From her earliest days in police training college, it was clear that she was going to make a name for herself in her chosen career. She was the outstanding recruit of her intake: physically fit, mentally agile, and singularly focused. No one worked harder than twenty-two-year-old Olivia Yates, and her efforts were rewarded at every stage of her career. She had aced every test and was presented with the prestigious best overall student award at her graduation ceremony. She then spent the next two years working as a police officer for the force, and she had excelled at it. She'd enjoyed the challenges that came with being a beat bobby, but her goal had always been to become a senior detective as part of the Serious Crime Squad, a role in which she felt she could make a real difference. To that end, after completing the mandatory two years as a police officer, Yates successfully applied for the role of trainee police detective with Brenton CID. Naturally, she was overjoyed—after six years of hard work, she was a detective. The future for Detective Yates looked promising, until, that is, DC Ulysses Hodge was assigned as her mentor.

A few hours after Donahue's death, Hodge had repurposed the whiteboard in the briefing room into what he called a "murder board". Prior to getting a job in CID, Yates had seen several of these "evidence boards", but most of them had been on television. She understood that old-school coppers often preferred old-school methods—and Hodge was definitely old-school—but wasn't this what computers were for? Though, if Hodge's computer screen was anything to go by, their primary purpose was to hold post-it notes. And even if the use of these boards had been standard practice, Yates was sure writing the word "murdered" alongside the deceased's name in bold capital letters, using a ghoulish red script, would be frowned upon.

The day after Donahue's death, Hodge had instructed Yates to find photos of the deceased and all the potential "perps" on the internet and print them off. He had then secured these to the whiteboard with a variety of colourful fridge magnets. At the centre of the board was a photo of Carl Donahue, which Yates had found on the parish council's website. The photos of the people Hodge had talked to earlier had been arranged around this. A photo of his chief suspect, Verity Meadows— which had been taken at a recent Women in Industry Awards ceremony—had been placed directly above the photo of the dead man, which was effectively fenced in by dozens of red arrows.

Hodge had written the name of each person above their photograph and drawn a single line between each photo and the photograph of the dead man. Each line was numbered clockwise, from one to seven. To the left of these photos were the corresponding numbers, and a summary of how they were connected to the man Hodge tellingly referred to as "The Victim".

Hodge removed his jacket and hung it over the back of his chair, unbuttoned his shirt cuffs and worked his silver sleeve garters over his biceps, revealing meaty forearms which were hairy enough to warrant regular combing. This was only the second time that Yates had seen Hodge adjust his shirtsleeves like this, and she knew it to be a sign that Hodge meant business.

Before commencing his lecture, Hodge picked up a brown, grease-spotted paper bag from his desk and peeled back the open end of the bag to reveal a partially eaten sausage roll. He examined the end of the snack before taking a bite. Still chewing, he turned his attention to the board.

'Right, Trainee Detective Constable, let's continue your journey towards enlightenment, shall we?'

Yates was sitting at a desk directly in front of the board, her notebook open on a fresh page, and a pen at the ready.

'Right then. Today's burning question is… Who murdered Carl Donahue?'

Yates raised her hand, finally feeling bold enough to ask a question that had been on her mind for some time.

'Yes, Yates?'

'Why are we treating this as a murder? We haven't had the results of the post-mortem back yet, have we?'

'The early bird catches the worm, Yates, and we're ahead of the flock for once.'

'Are we?' said Yates. 'It doesn't feel like it.'

'Well we are,' said Hodge irritably. 'And if we don't stay ahead, the Chief Super's going to call in the "big boys" before we've had a fair crack at it. But if we close this case, the people that matter will take notice—the same people who make decisions about promotions. I've been overlooked too many times, but that ends now, mark my words.'

'Okay,' said Yates, surprised by Hodge's unexpected outburst.

'And don't tell me you're not interested in bettering yourself, either,' said Hodge.

'Of course I am.'

'Good. Then let's get stuck in then, shall we?'

Hodge recapped everything they knew about each suspect and their connection to the victim until he came to Verity. He paused and studied her photo with such intensity it looked as though he was trying to read her thoughts. 'And of all of them,' he said, tapping the photo of Verity with his sausage roll, 'I fancy this one for it.'

'Really?' said Yates, subconsciously doodling a large question mark in her notebook.

'Absolutely,' said Hodge.

'But some of these others have known Donahue for over twenty years, whereas she's barely known him for twenty minutes.'

'Based on what?' asked Hodge.

'Based on everything we know right now,' said Yates, sensing that she was walking into a trap.

'That's right,' said Hodge, pleased that Yates had taken the bait. 'Based on what we know *right now*. So it's time we started digging a bit deeper then, isn't it?'

By the time Verity had finished populating the SUSPECTS board, it contained five names alongside three columns labelled "Means", "Motive", and "Opportunity"—a technique she'd lifted directly from the pages of her grandmother's first novel *Murdered by Midnight*. Under each column, Verity had made brief notes pertaining to the suspect, and the associated heading.

It was quickly agreed that both Brian and Tony had the means to kill Carl—assuming he was simply pushed out of the window. Rachel and Naomi were also likely to have the strength to push Carl out of the window, especially if he'd been caught unawares. They felt that Karina would struggle to do so, given that she had a history of knee and hip problems, but Verity felt they could not absolutely rule it out as a possibility, so on that basis, they felt that all five suspects were still in the running. As for motive, they felt that Tony and Karina shared a sufficiently strong motive for wanting to kill Donahue, closely followed by Brian, who they'd marked down a point or two because they felt if Brian could murder a love rival, he was more likely to do so when the pain of rejection was at its most intense. As for Rachel and Naomi, both Verity and Leeanne agreed that killing someone because they were—to use Leeanne's words—a "pervy old man", was a flimsy motive for murder. Finally, opportunity caused them the most problems, as they felt that all of them had equal opportunity to reach the storage room within a matter of seconds, given the close proximity of them all to Carl at the time of his death. Leeanne said that Karina was in reception at the time but factored in how close she was to the back stairs, which meant she was still a strong possibility. Verity had pointed out that call records would almost certainly show that Rachel was on the phone in the main office at the time, but it occurred to her that there was a remote possibility that she could have put the caller on hold then rushed upstairs and pushed Carl to his death before dashing back downstairs and continuing the telephone call, but this was such an absurd notion that she effectively dismissed it.

After much discussion, they concluded that they simply didn't have enough information to begin to narrow down their list of suspects.

'So, what do we do now then?' asked Leeanne.

'Well, you know these people far better than I do, and I think it's pretty clear that some of them aren't too keen to speak to me, so rather than risk getting more doors slammed in my face—or my face slammed into any doors—I'd like you to come with me to speak to them.'

'Okay, but what are we going to say to them?' Leeanne asked. 'We can't just ask them if they're murderers, can we?'

'We'll play it as though we're checking in to see how they are. We could take them a box of chocolates or some flowers or something to sweeten them up.'

'What type of chocolates?' Leeanne asked.

'I don't know. Whatever chocolates are on offer in the supermarket, I suppose.'

'They'd better not be white chocolates,' said Leeanne. 'They're disgusting. And no liqueurs, either. Yuck!'

Verity looked puzzled. 'But you won't be eating them, will you?'

'Why not?'

'Because… forget it. I tell you what, I'll buy you a box of your favourite chocolates while we're there. How's that?'

'Deal!' said Leeanne. 'So, who do we speak to next?'

'Well, I've already spoken to Brian, and I'm not sure how we're going to get past Karina's husband, so—'

'There's always God,' said Leeanne brightly.

Verity's speech systems stalled momentarily. 'I don't think even he can help us get past her husband, unless, of course, he's branched out into the assassination business.'

'No, dafty. I mean church. Karina always goes to church on Sunday, and Dennis—her husband—won't go anywhere near the place.'

'Really? I didn't have her down as a God-fearing woman,' said Verity. 'In fact, I rather suspect that God fears her.' She smiled at her own joke.

Leeanne didn't react.

Tough crowd, thought Verity.

'So, you think we should try to speak to her in church?'

'Why not? She's hardly going to start effing and jeffing in church, is she?'

'Good point,' said Verity, nodding appreciatively at Leeanne's logic.

'Okay, so if we're not going to get an opportunity to speak to Karina until Sunday, who do we speak to next?' asked Verity.

'We could just go through them in the order they are on the board?' said Leeanne.

'That's as good an idea as any.'

They both turned their attention to the names on the board.

Brian Butterworth
Karina Nolan
Rachel Eaves
Naomi Wilson
Tony Henley

'Right then. Let's see what Rachel has to say for herself, shall we?'

13

Rachel Eaves lived with her father in an ex-council house on the edge of Battley Common. The property was semi-detached and had been built in the 1960s. A Cypress tree, almost as tall as the house and still wrapped in Christmas lights, dominated the front garden.

The two women climbed out of Verity's car, and Leeanne led the way to the house.

A vintage caravan with flat tyres was parked on a paved area to the side of the house. A yellow transit van was alongside it, side door open, the radio playing a '90s hit from a "Madchester" band that Verity had disliked intensely back then, and her position on the matter hadn't changed in the intervening years. Leeanne pushed open a metal garden gate, which grated against its hinges, with Verity following closely behind.

A skinny man in his forties stepped out of the caravan. He was wearing a red bucket hat, a yellow tracksuit top, and blue tracksuit bottoms.

"Kinell, Leeanne!' he said, holding his hands before his face and making a show of averting his eyes. 'Does that top come with sunglasses? It's well trippy.'

Pretty rich coming from a man who looks like he's trying to blend in with a soft play area, Verity thought.

The man dropped his hands and smiled at Leeanne, revealing small grey teeth. 'Aright, our kid. How's it going?'

'Not so bad, Danny. How are you?'

'Yeah, sound. Who's the posh totty?'

'This is my friend Verity,' said Leeanne. 'And before you start, she's married.'

Danny eyed Verity up and gave her a cheeky wink. 'Alright, love?'

Verity was sure she felt her ovaries shrivel as some primitive defence mechanism kicked in.

'I'm very good, thank you,' she replied coolly.

He turned back to Leeanne. 'You after our kid, are ya?'

'Yeah.'

'Is this about that fella who died?' he asked, adopting a solemn demeanour.

Leeanne nodded.

'Bad news, that.'

'Yeah, it is,' said Leeanne, her chin lowered to her chest. 'We just want to see how she's doing, really.'

'Top banana. We had that Dibble round, mithering, a couple of days ago, but we've heard nowt since. Have they had a word with you, an' all?'

'They've spoken to all of us, I think,' Leeanne said, pointing between herself and Verity and then vaguely behind her to indicate those not present.

Danny removed his hat and ran his fingers through his thirty-year-old hairstyle. 'Do they know what happened to him?'

Leeanne shrugged. 'I don't know. I haven't heard anything either.'

He parted his mop of a fringe before putting his hat back on, then turned to the house and shouted up to the bedroom window.

'Rachel!'

There was no movement from upstairs. He shouted again, this time cupping his hands around his mouth. 'Rachel!'

He shook his head. 'She's probably still in bed, the lazy cow.'

'Don't worry, we can always come back,' said Verity.

A window, partially obscured by a huge satellite dish, flew open. Rachel's head shot out.

'What?' she said irritably.

'You've got visitors, you deaf cow!'

'I heard you. I was in the shower!'

'Again? Bloody hell, girl, you'll dissolve if you carry on.'

'At least I know how the shower works, you bloody soap dodger!'

'Don't you speak to me like that, you gobby trout!'

'Oh, get lost!'

Leeanne held her hand to her chest.

'No, not you, him,' she said. 'Gimme a minute and I'll be down.' She slammed the window.

Verity and Leeanne sat at a round breakfast table in the dilapidated kitchen, as Rachel poured herself a large bowl of cereal. Verity perched on the edge of a mismatched dining chair, trying to make as little contact with the seat as possible. The walls and ceiling had once been an off-white colour, but years of heavy smoking and food frying had stained them a sickly magnolia colour. One of the oak-effect kitchen units was missing a door, and another looked as though it were in imminent danger of falling off. A plate of half-eaten and long-forgotten cat food was on the floor, and a pile of plastic take-away containers were in a jumble on the draining board.

'Sorry about the state of the place,' said Rachel, as she poured milk into her bowl. 'My dad's supposed to be getting a payout from his old job, and when he does, he said he's going to get the kitchen sorted and help me with a deposit on a flat, so I can get out of this dump, but I'm not holding my breath—I know what he's like when he's got a few quid,' she said, miming a drinking session. She sat down next to Leeanne and adjusted her pink Playboy dressing gown. Ringlets of damp hair stuck to her forehead as she crunched and slurped her way through the sugary cereal. 'What brings you here, then?' she asked, her hand shooting up to her mouth to stop milk escaping. Verity looked away, desperately trying to find something to take her mind off Rachel's appalling table manners. On their journey here, it had been agreed that Leeanne would do most of the talking to begin with, to help put Rachel at ease.

'We just want to make sure you're alright, that's all,' said Leeanne.

'Yeah, I'm fine,' she said, losing a little of her breakfast down her dressing gown. 'Why wouldn't I be?'

'Well, with Carl and that, you know.'

Rachel shrugged. 'It's not my fault that he fell out of the window, is it? Probably a heart attack from all those pies.'

A possibility, Verity thought, especially as he'd got himself so worked up beforehand.

'Probably something like that, I'd imagine,' said Verity.

Rachel addressed Verity. 'Sorry, what's your name again —Felicity?'

'Verity.'

'That's the one. I knew it sounded posh,' said Rachel, before picking up her bowl and draining the last of the milk.

'You were there for a job interview, weren't you, for the parish clerk job?'

'That's right.'

Rachel took her bowl to the sink and dumped it on top of the other unwashed crockery, not bothering to rinse the bowl. 'I bet you wished you hadn't bothered now, don't you?'

'Yes, of course I do,' said Verity truthfully.

Rachel sat back in her chair and crossed her arms, and spent an uncomfortable amount of time looking Verity over with an air of disdain.

'I'm not being funny,' she said, causing Verity to brace herself for the inevitable "but" and the offensive remark that followed, 'but why is someone like *you* applying for a job like that?'

Somewhere deep inside of Verity, an alarm sounded battle stations. She knew that she couldn't afford to get her retaliation in first, as her very freedom hung in the balance, and regardless of Verity's opinion of Rachel, she could hold a vital piece of information that could get her off the hook.

'Well, to be brutally honest, I thought it would be a great way to get me out of the house, get to know the locals and become part of the community,' said Verity, the words sounded like something a poor candidate would say during a job interview. Rachel's expression spoke volumes.

'So, it would be a nice little hobby job for you, then? How lovely,' said Rachel, tightening her arms across her chest.

Verity's mouth opened, but no words were forthcoming, as she flicked through a series of possible responses and filtered out the inappropriate ones.

Aware of the building tension, Leeanne threw herself into the conversation again. 'Do you think it was an accident as well, then?'

'Course it was! Like I said, heart attack or he just tripped on something, silly sod,' said Rachel, her tension ebbing away.

'Yeah, probably,' said Leeanne.

'You said you were in the main office when it happened, didn't you?' said Verity.

'That's right. On the phone to Mr Higgins, listening to him going on about "marauding" gangs of youngsters who were up to no good, dropping litter right outside his place and kicking the heads off flowers near the memorial. I told him I'd call the Prime Minister and that seemed to satisfy him.'

Verity had already added this information to the white-board, but it was good to hear Rachel's account in more detail. As alibis went, this one was solid, as the call would be logged somewhere, and the caller would be able to corroborate Rachel's account. But Rachel still might know something useful, even if she wasn't aware if it herself.

'So you didn't see anything unusual beforehand that stuck in your mind, did you?' asked Verity.

'Didn't see anything? No, of course not. Like I told the police, I was in the office on my own at the time—had been for about fifteen minutes or so—Naomi was in the lavvy, turning herself inside out, after eating a kebab from that new chippy down from hers. So much for her being a vegetarian— or them having a five-star hygiene rating.'

'Oh dear,' said Verity, feeling a little queasy. 'And nothing before that, earlier in the day, or even recently? You didn't hear Carl arguing with anyone, or anything like that?'

'Nope. Nothing that springs to mind, anyhow. Now, you say, "out of the ordinary" but it wasn't out of the ordinary to hear raised voices when he was around. He was always shouting—loud, more than aggressive, mind—like the town crier he was.'

'And you can't think of anyone that would want to kill him?'

'No. He was no saint, but he was no devil either,' said Rachel. 'I reckon it was an accident, and that's all there is to it.'

'There was a rumour that he was having an affair with someone at the office.'

'Karina? That's not a rumour, that's a fact. But that's going back a while. He's married now, with little 'uns—or was. Poor things.'

Rachel sniffed and pressed the sleeve of her dressing gown against her nose, her eyes glossy and tinged pink.

Leeanne pulled a tissue out of her pocket and handed it to Rachel, who used it to blow her nose.

'I'd heard that they might have rekindled an old flame,' said Verity.

'Oh, really? Well, don't go believing everything you hear, especially not in this place. My gran used to joke that Hawbury ran on hot air from all the gossiping.'

'Didn't you say that he'd tried it on with you once?'

Rachel huffed. 'Years ago. He'd had a skinful, and he caught me hanging about under the mistletoe at the Christmas do, but I wasn't waiting for him, that's for sure. He tried to stick his tongue down my throat, so I kneed him where it hurts. He went down. End of,' she said, blinking. A tear appeared on her cheek. Leeanne produced another tissue and Rachel wiped her cheeks with it.

'Your grandmother was right—these places do run on hot air. But I'm not interested in rumours. I'm just trying to get a better understanding of what happened that day, and I can only do that with facts.'

Rachel turned to Verity and looked at her curiously. 'Why are you so interested in all this? You're not the police, and it's

A J FORD

their job to find out what went on, not some posh bird who happens to be blowing on through.'

'Excuse me? I'm not "blowing through". I own a property in the village, and I don't intend on going anywhere,' Verity said, surprised by how easily the lie came to her. 'And I understand it's the police's job to investigate this, but unfortunately the lead detective in this case seems to have it in for me, and I'm not going to stand by and do nothing while he tries to make me out to be a murderer!'

Verity took a breath, feeling better for getting that off her chest.

Rachel snorted.

'Hodge? Aren't you the lucky one?'

'I don't feel particularly lucky, I'll be honest,' said Verity.

'Don't worry about him, he'll be barking up another tree soon enough.'

'So people keep telling me, but that's easy to say when he hasn't got his sights set on you.'

Rachel shrugged.

They all sensed that the conversation had run its course. 'Well, thanks for talking to us,' said Verity. 'I appreciate it.'

As they left the house, they could hear Rachel's father singing 'There She Goes,' in a strained falsetto as he banged about in the caravan.

Rachel followed them out and stopped at the gate.

As Verity and Leeanne were getting into the car, Rachel called out after them, 'Do you know when Carl's funeral's going to be?'

'I don't know,' said Leeanne. 'I'm sure Tony will let us all know when he does.'

'Are you going to go?' asked Rachel.

'Yes,' said Leeanne.

122

'What about you?' she asked Verity.

'No. I don't know. I didn't know him. We'll see.'

'I hate funerals,' said Rachel.

'Let's hope it's the last for a while,' said Verity, as she buckled her seatbelt.

14

Verity rose early on Sunday to prepare for the day ahead. She had arranged to attend Sunday Service with Leeanne, with the intention of speaking to Karina without her husband being present.

As the time to leave for church neared, Verity became increasingly anxious about the meeting, so she busied herself around the house, catching up on some overdue chores to keep her mind off things. She had just finished scrubbing the bathroom to within an inch of its life when the alarm on her phone went off, indicating it was time to get ready.

Verity had laid out an outfit the night before but was now unsure of her choices. After a frantic few minutes of tearing through her wardrobe, she left the house wearing white chinos, a crisp white shirt, lilac jacket, and navy pumps. A small navy shoulder bag was the only designer label on show. It was a fine morning, and the weather forecast suggested it wasn't going to rain, so Verity had decided to walk to church as it saved her the embarrassment of driving that car again.

When she arrived at the church, she stood outside the

gates waiting for Leeanne to arrive. They'd agreed to meet just before eleven, and the church clock showed it was almost ten to. A steady trickle of worshippers passed her by, bidding her good morning, before whispering conspiratorially about a subject most unsuitable for discussion on hallowed ground. Verity had expected it, of course, but woe betide the first person she caught saying anything out of turn about her. She was getting lost in thoughts of bloody vengeance and swift retaliation when someone leapt out from behind the gatepost.

'Boo!'

Despite the juvenile nature of Leeanne's surprise attack, Verity was startled. It was only Leeanne's quick reflexes and Verity's poor aim that saved her from getting a smack on the side of the head.

'Good God, you scared the… wits out of me then,' said Verity, mindful that she was near a place of worship.

Leeanne was practically doubled over, her hands on her knees, consumed by a most unflattering laugh.

Unamused, Verity took Leeanne by the elbow and led her unceremoniously to the main entrance, her companion still laughing even as they entered the church.

Inside, the church was much of a muchness. Rows of wooden pews ran either side of the nave, and the congregation—which was scarcely a quarter of a capacity crowd—had filed into the front five rows.

Verity had managed to bring Leeanne back to her senses and asked her to subtly identify Karina from the backs of the rows of heads. She was sitting in the second row from the front, in the middle of the pew. The third row was fully occupied, save for one space, almost directly behind Karina. An elderly lady with hair like a dandelion clock had placed her handbag on the vacant seat next to her. The unoccupied seats on this side would put them too far away from Karina to be of any use, so Verity made a bold move. Dragging Leeanne behind her, she shuffled along the third row, apologising as she went, leaving much head shaking and tutting in her wake.

When they reached the one vacant seat, the old dear looked up from her prayer book. 'Sorry, this one's taken,' she whispered.

'It is now, budge up,' said Verity, picking up the woman's handbag and placing it on her lap.

'But my husband is sitting there,' the woman said, incredulous.

'He's not though, is he?'

'He's just gone to answer the call of nature. He'll be back in a minute.'

The muttering around them was almost loud enough to drown out the organist.

Ignoring the disapproving comments, Verity sat down.

'Look,' she whispered, 'my friend has had a vision, and God has told her that she needs to sit in this exact seat, right now, and you wouldn't want to get on the wrong side of him now, would you? What with you being so close to meeting him and everything.'

The old lady was taken aback by this, but she stood up without comment and made her way to the end of the row. Verity and Leeanne sat in their hijacked seats. Verity hung her head and took the opportunity to offer up a quick prayer, asking for forgiveness for what she'd just done, on the off chance that someone was listening.

As the last-minute arrivals settled into their seats, an unspoken conversation took place between Verity and Leeanne. They communicated in a series of frantic nods and eye movements, forming exaggerated word shapes with their mouths.

Go on then!

You do it!

No, YOU!

Just do it!

To put an end to it, Leeanne tapped Karina on the shoulder nearest to Verity, and quickly bowed her head, as though in silent contemplation.

Karina turned around sharply. Upon seeing Verity, her face soured.

'Oh, for God's sake,' she said in a whisper of sorts. 'Dennis said you'd been round, causing a nuisance. What do you want?'

'I just want to ask you a few questions, that's all,' said Verity, in a hushed tone.

'What about?'

'About Carl. I just want a few minutes of your time—'

'No. My husband's already said it all. Now leave me be!' she said, no longer attempting to keep her voice down.

Verity looked up. The vicar, standing behind the lectern, straightened up and surveyed the diminished flock, her gaze lingering on the pair. Verity looked down at the floor, old-fashioned Catholic guilt catching a flame deep within her.

It was now or never, she reasoned.

Another shoulder tap.

'What?' said Karina, through gritted teeth.

The vicar cleared her throat.

Verity took a breath, then hit her with it.

'Were you having an affair with Carl when he died?'

Heads on either side of the women turned to Karina, keen to hear her response, which was delivered with unexpected physicality as she turned and pounced on Verity, who was caught unawares.

'Leave. Me. Alone!' Karina said, as she lashed out at Verity.

'Get off me, you tart!'

There were gasps from the congregation. One or two younger attendees began surreptitiously recording the fight, and were soon rewarded for their journalistic instincts, as the squabble escalated into a saloon-style brawl.

Fighting blindly, Verity swung a fist upwards, in the vague direction of the source of the blows that were raining down on her. She felt her fist connect solidly against something fleshy and heard a scream, but the frequency and intensity of the blows did not diminish. The woman Verity had struck, who was not Karina, fell back into the lap of the man next to her. And from there, a chain reaction spread through those who'd been unwilling or unable to flee the violence. Many of the men present—and a surprising number of women—took this opportunity to settle some old scores: border disputes, bad debts, inconsiderate parking, noisy neighbours, balls kicked against walls, discovered affairs, spurned advances, unreturned garden tools, stolen cake recipes, and so on.

The vicar, now crouched behind the lectern, begged these sinners to come to their senses, but her words were drowned out by the sound of old scores being settled. A blue kneeler embroidered with a white dove flew past the vicar at a frightening velocity. Under fire, she dropped to the ground and made her way to the relative safety of the pulpit.

A pew toppled over nearby, reinvigorating a cluster of flagging combatants. In the chaos, Leeanne fought to free herself from the clutches of a well-meaning man who'd held her back when she'd tried to intervene. A well-placed blow took him out of action, allowing Leeanne to go to the aid of her beleaguered friend. She pulled an exhausted Karina off her friend before wrapping an arm around Verity and pushing her way through the knot of bodies, shielding her from the worst of the blows as she went. She'd just broken free of the crowd when an unseen person grabbed her from behind.

Leeanne was able to propel Verity into the aisle before falling to the ground herself. Her cheek pressed against cold red tiles, and she took in the carnage that was going on around her. Something silver caught Leeanne's attention. She sprang to her feet and turned to face her attacker—a man from her past who wouldn't take no for an answer. 'Remember me?' he said, an unsettling grin on his face. Wild eyes flicked from his old flame to the large metal collection plate she was holding. His expression changed as realisation dawned too late.

Thank goodness they hadn't gone contactless yet, Leeanne thought, as she brought the collection plate down over her assailant's head with a clang.

From behind the pulpit, the vicar reached up and turned on the microphone. Setting the volume to full, she addressed her wayward flock. From above the heads of the congregation, a voice boomed.

'Please, for the love of God, stop!'

By the time the police arrived at the church, the fighting had burnt itself out. Most of the walking wounded had made their way into the church grounds. Upon seeing a police van pull up, punched-out parishioners turned their faces away and quickened their pace. Leeanne had guided Verity out of the church through a narrow side door, which opened onto the graveyard. After a short walk down a country lane, they arrived at the Pig & Pickle pub.

Leeanne gave the barkeeper a nod as she and Verity ducked through into the snug.

'Two medicinal G and Ts, please, Chas.'

The server—a tall, tattooed woman with jagged pink hair and a pierced nose—free-poured two generous measures of gin into glasses and topped them off with a dash of tonic water, ice, and a slice.

'I'll get these,' said Verity, looking about her for her shoulder bag, which was nowhere to be seen.

'I think I've lost my bag,' she said. Her face dropped when she realised where it would be. 'I must have dropped it in church,' she said, shaking her head.

'Well, we're not going back there now to look for it, that's for sure,' said Leeanne.

'That's seven-eighty, please, darling.'

'Thanks, Chas, you're an angel,' said Leeanne, passing her a ten pound note and telling her to keep the change.

Leeanne sat down. 'That could have gone better,' she observed, taking a sip of her drink, which was potent enough to strip paint. Verity would have nodded in agreement, but her head ached too much. She took a generous slug of gin and spluttered. 'Hellfire, how many measures are in that?'

'Enough to do the job,' came the reply.

Her throat and mouth anaesthetised from the first slug, Verity felt brave enough to throw the second one back.

'What do we do now then?' Leeanne asked, her voice half an octave lower due to the potent drink.

Verity waggled a finger in her ear, her eardrums now uncomfortably warm, thanks to the sudden influx of alcohol that had just entered her bloodstream.

'I honestly don't know. As much as I'd like to throw the towel in, I can't. I wouldn't blame you if you did, though.'

'Not bloody likely,' said Leeanne, trying to blink her vision back into focus.

Verity rested her hand on the back of Leeanne's. 'Thanks. That's really good of you, but I don't want you to get into any bother on my account.'

'Bother? Hodge, you mean? Pfft. I'd like to see him try it,' said Leeanne.

'Based on what I saw of your performance earlier, I'd quite like to see him try it, too,' said Verity, smiling as she imagined how such an encounter might pan out. As Verity was lost in thought, Leeanne signalled to Chas for another round of medicinal gin and tonics.

Verity made short work of the next drink and was pleased to note that its medicinal properties had completely alleviated any aches or pains she might have had, or indeed any sensation other than a warm buzz that enveloped her. After an interesting return journey from the ladies, Verity tried to get back up on her stool and thought better of it. Instead, she sat on the end of a long bench seat in a vacant booth and fell backwards, giggling.

'We just had a fight in church. We are so going to burn in hell,' said Verity.

Leeanne sat on the bench opposite her inebriated friend. 'I'm not going to hell—they won't have me.'

Despite having developed a taste for Chas's legendary medicinal measures, Leeanne wisely ordered two large filter coffees. At first, Verity was reluctant to drink the coffee, insisting that they should have one for the road, but she eventually conceded.

Verity's head was a little clearer after the coffee, and after some discussion the two came up with a foolproof Plan B: if you can't go through an obstacle, you simply have to go around it.

15

Verity woke up on her sofa, with no idea what day it was, or why she'd slept downstairs in her clothes. She sat up, massaged her face, yawned, and stretched. A wall clock showed it was approaching six o'clock, but Verity wasn't sure if it was a.m. or p.m. until she checked her phone. Sunday, 6 p.m. She shuffled into the kitchen, took an upturned mug from the draining board, and placed it in the coffee machine. From the rotary holder, she selected a black coffee pod, which promised to deliver an almost lethal dose of caffeine, and dropped it into her machine. She pressed the button to wake the machine up, thinking that it would be handy to have such a button herself. While she waited for the coffee machine, she propped herself up on her elbows and yawned again, recalling a surreal dream about monks with large moustaches fighting inside a monastery.

Verity's eyes shot open. 'Oh God,' she said. *The church. That was real!*

She made her coffee and sat down. She'd barely taken her first sip when there was a knock at her door. And it wasn't a polite knock, either. In Verity's experience, it was a knock used by impatient couriers, debt collectors, and police officers. She looked through the spyhole in the door and was unsurprised to see Hodge, looking even more convex than was usual. Behind him was a tall, dark-haired woman in a dark grey trouser suit. Reluctantly, she opened the door.

'What do you want?'

'Well, that's no way to greet an old friend, is it?' Hodge said in mock indignation. 'I thought we'd be getting on much better since our little chat in the supermarket. You remember that, don't you?' His eyes narrowed.

'When you were caught shoplifting, you mean?' Verity touched her chin and tilted her head. 'Yes, I remember it frequently, and I will continue to do so for a very long time.'

A muscle rippled in Hodge's jaw, and colour rose up his neck. There was a brief silence as he swallowed his anger. Verity wanted nothing more than to close the door on him, but she was enjoying watching him experience a little discomfort.

'Well?' said Verity.

'Yes, I'm not so bad, thanks. Yourself?' said Hodge.

Verity rolled her eyes. 'What do you want?'

'Did you actually just roll your eyes at me?' He turned to Yates. 'Did you see that? Unbelievable.'

'I haven't got all day, Detective. Now kindly state your business or get off my property.'

'Tetchy, aren't we?'

'No, not tetchy, I'm busy.'

'Well, aren't you going to invite us in?'

Verity considered this.

'Must I? I've read *Dracula*, and I know that nothing good comes of inviting your kind in.'

133

Yates put a hand to her mouth and made a small squeaking sound. Hodge gave her a withering look.

'It's entirely up to you, of course, Mrs Meadows, but you may have noticed that my voice carries, and we wouldn't want your neighbours overhearing, would we?'

Verity stood away from the door and waved them in reluctantly.

'Very cosy,' said Hodge as he took the place in, pretending to be taking an interest in the decor, when in reality he was already scanning the room for the telltale signs that he was in the presence of a hardened criminal—misappropriated office stationery, branded coffee shop mugs, IKEA pencils, that sort of thing.

Verity looked about to see if any of her neighbours were watching before closing the door hurriedly.

They stood in the lounge. As was customary, he introduced his colleague. 'You and I are already acquainted, of course, but this is Trainee Detective Constable Yates.'

Trainee. Yates was used to the slight. Any other officer in the country would have omitted the word trainee, but not Hodge. He'd likened it to displaying L plates, and that was his justification for doing so, but the truth was far simpler—he liked people to know their place, and if that was below him, then so much the better.

The female detective held out her warrant card and gave Verity a nod. 'Y' alright?'

In stark contrast to Hodge, she seemed… human.

'Trainee Detective, you say?'

'That's right,' said Hodge, answering for her, as he often did.

Verity addressed Hodge. 'And you're her training officer?'

'That's correct,' he said.

Verity gave Yates a sympathetic look. 'God help you, kid.'

Yates pushed her tongue into her cheek and looked about the place. She envied Verity. It was so nice to hear someone say things out loud that she could only say in her head—or scream into her pillow.

'Well, sit down, there's no point in you standing round like bowling pins,' said Verity, snatching up the throw she'd just been sleeping under. The detectives sat. Verity took the armchair opposite.

'I'd offer you a coffee, but I don't have any,' she said, taking a long drink of her freshly brewed coffee.

Childish, but very satisfying.

Verity noticed that the shoulder bag she'd dropped at the church now sat between the police officers.

So that's what this is about, Verity thought.

'Come on then, let's have it,' she said.

'As you are no doubt aware, a serious incident took place during Sunday Service this morning. And we believe you are a witness to the violent disorder that took place. Is that correct?' he asked, holding up exhibit A: one small, navy-blue shoulder bag. Designer brand. Impractical. Eye-wateringly expensive.

'That's right,' she said, reaching out for her handbag. 'Not so much a witness, though—more a victim.'

'A victim is also a witness, Mrs Meadows,' said Hodge. 'As is a perpetrator.'

Here we go again.

'Hang on a minute,' she said, standing up and plucking the suspended bag from Hodge's grasp. 'Are you saying that you think this is all my doing as well?' She glared at him—daring him to say yes.

Hodge shook his head. 'If I thought this was your doing, we'd be having a far less amicable conversation down the road by now.'

Verity calmed down and took her seat. 'So why are you

here?' she asked, as she checked the contents of her bag were all present. 'I can't imagine it's because you've been promoted to the lost property division so soon?'

'Your wit knows no beginning, Meadows,' said Hodge.

Touché.

'We'd just like to hear your side of things,' he continued. 'To ensure that the right people are brought to justice, as we are duty bound to do.'

Verity tossed her head scornfully.

'So, when you're ready, my colleague will take a few notes, for our reference.'

Yates took out a fresh notebook and popped the lid off a new biro, and scribbled on the inside back cover, to get the ink flowing.

She cleared her throat and began. 'So, in your own words, can you take us through the events that took place in St Crispin's this morning, please?' Yates had a warm northern accent. Verity couldn't place it exactly, but she sounded like one of the people in the call centres she used to have to speak to when she had a problem with her mobile phone or her broadband.

Verity ran through the events as best as she could remember them, though she played down Karina's involvement quite considerably, justifying it to herself later by telling herself that it would only make her life more difficult as she continued to investigate Donahue's death, if the feud between the two of them continued.

After Verity had finished giving her version of events, Yates placed the notebook and pen back in her inside pocket.

Hodge sat back and steepled his fingers and rested his chin on his thumbs—an affectation he'd recently adopted to convey a sense of deep concentration. He closed his eyes and took a breath.

'A very interesting account, Mrs Meadows. Quite different from what we're hearing.'

'Fancy that,' said Verity. 'Come on then, what is it you're hearing?'

'That you've never attended a service at St Crispin's before, and the moment you arrived, you made directly for Karina Nolan and started interrogating her about our ongoing investigation into the death of Carl Donahue. And when Mrs Nolan didn't give you the answers you wanted, you proceeded to set about her person, in a sustained and unprovoked attack.'

Verity instantly regretted playing down Karina's part in all this.

'And this is the account of Karina Nolan, no doubt?'

'And others.'

'I see. And these "others" will be friends of hers, I take it? Well, funnily enough, a friend of mine will tell you it was Karina who attacked me.'

'That's not what you just said, Mrs Meadows,' said Yates. She took out her notebook and referred to her notes. 'You said, and I quote, "I asked Karina if it was convenient to talk and she said no it wasn't, and when I pressed her on it, she pushed me away and told me to eff off", end quote.'

Verity was furious with herself for not telling the truth in the first place, and with Karina and her cronies for concocting such a bare-faced lie.

'I only said that because I didn't want to cause any further trouble. God knows we've all had enough of that to last us a lifetime. It was she who assaulted me, and that's the truth.'

'It is really? Given your penchant for telling lies, it's very difficult to tell, I'm afraid.'

'I'll swear to it,' said Verity.

'You can save that for the courtroom, Meadows.'

'What do mean by that?' said Verity, leaping out of her seat.

'Do you intend to press charges against me? Because if you do, I'll lawyer up and sue you for harassment, then I'll press charges against that old slapper for GBH, and sue her for slander, for good measure.'

Hodge remained calm in spite of Verity's outburst.

'Can I give you some advice, Mrs Meadows?'

'No.'

Hodge stood up, indicating that Yates should do the same. 'Well, I'm going to anyway,' he said. 'Stay well out of my way and leave this investigation to the professionals.'

'Certainly,' said Verity, folding her arms indignantly. 'Do you know what time they'll be arriving?'

Hodge shook his head and sighed. 'I mean it, Meadows. I don't want to see you anywhere near this investigation. Do you understand?'

Verity ignored him and opened the front door. 'Goodbye, detectives.'

Verity stood on her doorstep once they'd left the house and watched them like a hawk.

As Hodge closed the gate, he left Verity with a warning. 'Remember, if you so much as sneeze near this investigation again, I'll be on you like a ton of bricks. Understand?'

They got in the car and pulled away, Hodge maintaining eye contact for the duration. Verity shouted after them, 'I'll sneeze where I bloody well like!'

The detectives' car had barely rounded the first bend in the road when Hodge instructed Yates to pull over into a lay-by.

'What's wrong?' Yates asked.

'Nothing.'

Yates stopped the car, and Hodge got out.

'Why are we stopping here?' Yates asked as she lowered her window.

She watched him in the mirrors as he took out a small rucksack and slung it over one shoulder. Then he pulled out a green walking jacket and shook it.

'Fieldwork,' he said, approaching the driver's door, handing the jacket to his trainee.

Yates looked down into the footwell. She didn't fancy trudging through mud in the shoes she was wearing.

'Are we going into an actual field?'

'No. You're in the car, I'm in the field.'

'Why, what are we doing?'

'We've got Meadows stirred up rather nicely. If she's going to do anything, she's not going to hang about. I'm going to watch the back of her place and you're going to watch the front. If she makes a move, I'll give you a shout and you can follow her at a distance, so make sure you've got your radio turned up.'

Yates looked at the jacket. 'So, what's that for then, if I'm in the car?'

'What did they actually teach you when you did that "professional policing" degree?'

Every time he mentioned her degree, he enclosed it within air quotes.

'Next to nothing about leisurewear, that's for sure.'

'It's a disguise. She's already seen the car, but if she's looking out for a tail, she'll be expecting to see both of us in it. There's a pair of sunglasses and a cap in the pockets, put them on and pull up behind the bus stop over there, and wait for my signal.'

Hodge had positioned himself in a field behind Verity's cottage. He was crouched behind a section of crumbling drystone wall, watching the target's home through a pair of binoculars. He'd tied his jacket around his waist to hide the fact that he'd torn the backside out of his trousers climbing over a stile.

He was on his third energy bar in thirty minutes when he saw movement at the bedroom window.

He picked up his radio. 'Movement at the bedroom window on the south side of the property. It looks like our target is getting changed.' Hodge averted his gaze for a few seconds, thinking that Meadows should really close her bedroom curtains.

'Okay…' said Yates to herself, uncertain what she should do with this information. She keyed the mic. 'Roger.' A moment later, Hodge spoke again.

'She's downstairs now. It looks like she's picked something up and is moving towards the front door. Stand by.'

A few seconds passed.

'She's out the door. The hen has flown the coop, I repeat, the hen has flown the coop. Go. Go. Go!'

16

Verity had originally intended to call upon Naomi Wilson the next morning, but Hodge's insistence that she stay well away from the investigation had made it clear to her that time was of the essence. This impromptu visit meant she wouldn't have Leeanne as backup, and this was playing on her mind until she reminded herself that it was only the incompetent detective who believed they were dealing with a murder. Much to Verity's surprise, Naomi lived alone in a new three-bed detached house, on a development called "Badgers Rise". Verity thought this sounded like the title of a low-budget horror movie. Despite its dreadful name, most of the houses on this estate had been snatched up as soon as they went onto the market, long before a single brick had been laid, as they were some of the cheapest homes in the area.

Leeanne had told her that Naomi was only just able to afford the place, as she'd originally been buying the property with her then fiancé, Simon. But soon after Naomi had put down the deposit, using her own money, a video of Simon and "Sudsy Sue" at a foam party in Magaluf had appeared on Facebook, and brought their engagement to a swift end. Leeanne then went into explicit detail about the video, and the fact that the mortgage was now in Naomi's parents' names, and how Naomi was often behind with her payments to her parents, which had caused a blazing row when her father had caught her "pissing his money down the drain" at a cocktail bar, one night. The level of detail Leeanne was able to provide made Verity wonder if her friend didn't have access to a secret network of spies.

Verity parked in the visitor parking, checked her notebook to ensure she had the correct address, and walked over to the house.

'Oh, hello, I'd heard you were doing the rounds,' said Naomi, as she opened the door. 'Come in.'

Verity was taken aback. 'Are you sure? I won't take up much of your time,' she said, wiping her feet on a doormat which read, "COME IN IF YOU HAVE GIN". Cream carpet had been fitted throughout the house. Verity used a small table in the hallway to support herself as she removed her shoes and took the place in. The ground floor was bisected by a set of central stairs. On the left was a kitchen diner, and there was a full-length lounge on the right. The interior had been decorated nicely. It had some of the touches you'd expect to see in a show home; a glitzy mirror above the fireplace; a chrome fruit bowl, complete with plastic fruit; a large clock stencilled onto the kitchen wall. Verity hadn't been upstairs, but she was willing to bet that the master bedroom had some inspirational message written above the bed—LIVE, LAUGH, LOVE—that kind of thing. Photos of all these details would be all over Naomi's "Insta", no doubt. But for all the cute designer touches, there were things that made the place feel unfinished —an empty magazine rack in the lounge; a dusty, vacant flower vase in the hallway; two empty picture hooks either side of the fireplace, from which photos of a young couple had once hung, Verity guessed.

'This is lovely,' said Verity as she walked into the kitchen diner.

'Aww. Thanks,' said Naomi, sitting down at a two-seater breakfast table; a copy of a gossip magazine lay open atop it, next to a large glass of wine.

'Take a seat,' said Naomi, closing the magazine.

'Thanks.'

Naomi was a striking young woman. She had lustrous black hair which was so dark it had a hint of blue in it. Large, emerald green eyes, emphasised by soft-smoke eyeliner, stood out against her pale complexion.

'I take it this is about what happened with Mr Donahue,' said Naomi.

'Yes. As you've obviously heard, I've been speaking to a few of the others, trying to get a better understanding of what happened—'

'I've heard, alright. What happened in the church was well mad!'

'That was nothing to do with me, I can assure you.'

'Have you seen the videos? They're all over the internet. There's one of you getting punched by Karina that's got about a hundred thousand likes already.'

Verity despaired of humanity. Naomi's comment reinforced her belief that social media would bring about the downfall of the species. How, in a civilised society, could one hundred thousand people "like" a video of someone being assaulted?

'Do you want to see it?' asked Naomi, picking up her mobile phone.

'No, thank you,' said Verity.

Deflated, Naomi put her phone down.

'Is this because Hodge has been onto you about what happened—saying he thinks you pushed Carl and that?'

'Pretty much, yes. And I think we're all of the opinion that it was nothing more than a tragic accident.'

Naomi picked up her glass and ran a thumb through the condensation on the outside of it, before taking a drink. Verity noticed that her nail polish was the same colour as her eyes.

'Do you think it was an accident?' Naomi asked.

'Yes, on the balance of probability, I do,' said Verity.

'I'm not being funny or anything, but if you think it was an accident, then why are you here?'

Verity took some time to consider the best way to phrase it, given that her previous approaches had delivered less than spectacular results.

'I know the police will have taken their statements from everyone, but I'd like to go over it, in case they've overlooked anything—just for my own peace of mind.'

'I get it. In case they try to charge you with anything?'

'That's right.'

'Okay. But can I ask you a question first?'

Verity hadn't expected to be quizzed herself.

'Of course. Go ahead,' she said, feeling inexplicably nervous.

'You were there for a job interview, weren't you—for the parish clerk job?'

Verity nodded. 'Yes. Why do you ask?'

Naomi took another drink of wine—a hefty swig, this time.

'Well, I don't want to be rude, but you don't look like you need the money, and that job would make a lot of difference to someone like me.'

It took Verity a moment to register what Naomi meant.

'Oh. You'd applied for the job as well?'

Naomi nodded.

Of course. Naomi was judging this book by its designer cover, and not the contents of its bank balance. It was true that Verity didn't need the money—she was applying for the job to give herself something to do, after all—but at the time she hadn't considered that if she were successful in her application, she would be depriving someone else of the opportunity. Ordinarily, Verity couldn't give a single hoot about things like that as she firmly believed that the best candidate should get the job, not the neediest, but she took on board what Naomi said, and felt a twinge of guilt.

'Well, I wouldn't worry about that now. I certainly won't be pursuing my application.'

'That's alright then,' Naomi said, pressing a hand to her chest. At that moment, her phone rang. She looked down at the caller ID and stood up.

'Sorry, one sec,' she said, as she made her way out through the kitchen door and stood on the small square of patio slabs outside the kitchen window, turning to face the garden.

Verity made good use of her time alone, looking around for things which gave her a better sense of who this person was.

Naomi used the fridge door to organise her life. Fridge magnets secured bills, receipts, appointment cards, flyers, and takeaway menus. Ever curious, Verity scanned the jumble of papers. The only items of note were a utility bill marked FINAL REMINDER, and a leaflet for Clebe Cosmetic. Verity had visited the neighbouring village of Clebe a couple of times and was not a fan of the place.

Two wipe-clean weekly planners, titled WEEK AHEAD and MEAL PLANNER, were secured to the side of the fridge. The meals on the planner weren't particularly gastronomic— mostly something and chips or one-pot pasta dishes.

Assuming this board was kept up to date, today's meal had been wiped off the board.

The Week Ahead board had three entries for the week:

Monday: Dentist—2:30

A dentist with a sense of humour, thought Verity.

Wednesday: Hair—11:00

Thursday: Cons. Dr Masoud. CC—11:30

Verity assumed that CC stood for Clebe Cosmetic and guessed that Naomi was considering cosmetic surgery. Though why she would do such a thing was beyond Verity, as she was perfect as she was.

Naomi entered, concluding her conversation with, 'Okay. I'll see you in a bit,' before retaking her seat. 'Sorry about that.'

'It's okay. Look, if you're expecting company, we can always do this some other time,' said Verity.

'No. It's fine. This won't take too long, will it?'

'No, not at all.'

Verity picked up the conversation from where she'd left off. 'How long have you worked for the council?'

'Just over a year.'

'Okay. So long enough to know everyone pretty well?'

'I suppose so, yes.'

'Would you mind telling me a bit about them?' said Verity, her notebook at the ready and, after reassurance that the notes were only for Verity's benefit, Naomi obliged, talking freely, with Verity giving her only the occasional prompt.

Brian was a grumpy old so-and-so, who didn't have much to do with anyone in the office other than Tony or Carl, and since the incident with Karina, he'd taken to eating his lunch outside on good days or in his car if it was raining. He was no grumpier with Carl than he was with any of the others, but he often brought boxes of veg in from his garden when he had more than he could use, and left them in the staff kitchen.

Karina was nice—despite what you might think, she added. She often brought cakes or biscuits in for everyone. She loved baking but was watching her figure—and she always brought in a bit extra for her "growing lad", Carl. Despite what had gone on in the past, she still spoke to Brian, even though he didn't say a great deal in return.

Rachel was fine. They didn't really have much in common, apart from their age and taste in men. When Naomi had first started there, they'd gone out together after work, but that died off after a while, as they invariably fought over the same men. Apart from that time Rachel had kneed Carl "right where it hurts" she'd got on fine with him in work, though she'd confided in Naomi that she still thought he was a bit of a sex pest.

Everyone loved Tony, she said. He was her favourite boss ever. He would often take them all out for meals or drinks and often pick up the bill—especially if they'd gone somewhere expensive. Even Brian warmed up on those nights. She knew that Carl still owed Tony money for house improvements or something, but it didn't seem to be an issue for Tony, who'd inherited a tidy sum when his parents had died.

Leeanne lit the room up wherever she went, due in part to her attire. There seemed to be an unwritten rule that the more prestigious the event, the louder her outfit. Like most men who knew her, Carl was smart enough not to mess with Leeanne. Her reputation as something of a terrier was well known. When Verity heard this, she couldn't help but smile. She'd seen flashes of it herself, and it endeared Leeanne to her all the more. The consensus was that Leeanne was a force to be reckoned with—a fiercely loyal, free spirit, who would always remain an enigma to some.

Carl had been summed up pretty well by his relationship with others—a loudmouthed lech, though Verity was aware that her assessment of the man was being coloured by her own experience of him. Dead or otherwise, it was hard for her to warm to the man.

'And what about you?' Verity asked when she'd finished.

'What do you mean?'

'What about your relationship with Carl? I think you'd said he was a bit creepy when we were all interviewed. Is that a fair assessment?'

Naomi looked down at the magazine and started flicking through the pages. 'I don't like to say, really. It's not nice, is it —saying mean things about him.'

'Your words can't hurt him now,' said Verity.

'Yeah, I know, but still—it's not very nice.'

Verity remained silent. After a moment, Naomi spoke.

'He was just a bit—you know—creepy around other women. Always making jokes and that. He was always saying "as the actress said to the bishop" after everything. Which was funny for a bit, but it got a bit much after a while. Then there were rumours going around about him and Karina, but I didn't see anything myself, so I wouldn't want to accuse him of anything—besides, it's not my business what they get up to in their own time.'

Verity nodded sympathetically. Sensing that she'd got as much as she could about the group dynamic without making this a formal interrogation, Verity directed the conversation to where Naomi was when the incident took place.

'I was in the toilet when it happened. I had a bit of an upset tummy, and I was in there for quite a while.'

'That's right,' Verity said. 'Rachel said you'd had a dodgy kebab or something?'

'Well, that's what I told her. The truth is, I get really bad IBS when I'm nervous, and I'd got myself all worked up about the interview I was supposed to be having after you, and it set me off. I've got tablets for it, but they take a while to kick in. I told Rachel it was probably a kebab because I didn't want her knowing I was nervous because she was going for the job too, and I thought she might make me worse if she knew.'

'You were in there for quite a while then?'

'Yes, about twenty minutes or more, I'd say. God, it's so embarrassing. I hate using the loo in work at the best of times, but sometimes you've got no choice, have you?'

'When you've got to go, you've got to go,' said Verity. 'Did you hear anything at all when you were in there—from outside the cubicle, I mean?'

'I did hear a bit of shouting.'

Verity assumed this was when Carl had started going berserk in Tony's office. The very thought of it made her palms sweat, even now.

'Then I heard heavy footsteps on the stairs, so I guessed that was Carl, and it sounded like he was talking all kinds of nonsense. I tried to listen to what he was saying, but I couldn't make any sense of it. It was like he was on drugs or something.'

Verity jumped on this. 'How many people did you hear on the stairs?'

'Just Carl, as far as I could tell.'

'Then after that?' Verity asked, becoming increasingly animated, as though she were on the brink of a revelation. Verity watched Naomi look up and to the right as she reviewed the memory of that fateful event.

'Then I heard glass break…'

'And then?'

'And then I heard your car alarm go off and a woman screaming.'

Verity was pretty sure that it was she who'd screamed.

In the seconds that followed, both of them were trapped in

the awful memory of the last few moments of Carl Donahue's life.

Soon after, aware that Naomi had other plans, Verity thanked her and said she'd see herself out. She closed the door behind her without looking back, before getting into her car and driving away, unaware that she was being observed from a discreet distance.

Verity had been disappointed that the conversation hadn't uncovered any startling revelations, initially, but she left with a real sense that she was on the cusp of a breakthrough. She had made her way back through the high street, which almost certainly wasn't the shortest way home, but it was the route she was most familiar with, which meant she was unlikely to get lost. At this time of night, the high street was quiet. A few couples were making their way to the pub for an evening meal, their arms interlinked. As Verity was about to turn off the main drag through the village, she caught sight of a familiar figure, a man in a dark blue blazer and blue jeans—Tony. He was carrying a bunch of what looked like garage-bought flowers and heading in the direction Verity had come from. Verity slowed to watch him, trying to keep track of him in the Morris's little round side mirror. She saw him stop outside the fish and chip shop and peer in—looking to check the opening hours, she thought—before continuing his journey up the road. When she turned to see where Tony went, she very nearly hit a parked car. By the time she'd brought the car to a stop, to allow herself to track him safely, he'd disappeared from view, but it wasn't difficult to put the pieces of this puzzle together.

So that's who you were meeting, then, she thought. *You kept that quiet, didn't you?*

17

Verity stood in her garden, talking to Leeanne on the telephone as the sun kissed the horizon. Her words were little more than a whisper as she arranged a clandestine meeting with her friend later that night.

Later, two figures, clad from head to toe in black, stood outside The Old Courthouse. Verity wore black joggers, hoodie, trainers, and a D&G baseball cap. Leeanne wore a pair of Gary's work trousers, legs rolled up and cinched tight at the waist with a brown leather belt, and a black polo shirt with the name of Gary's company plastered across the back of it.

'If you're wearing that, I'd love to see what Gary's wearing,' said Verity.

'I didn't have any choice. I don't own any black clothes, do I. I'm not a Goth, you know!'

'Shhh. Keep your voice down,' said Verity, her nerves set on edge by the thought of anyone overhearing them.

Verity recalled that Brian had said only the CCTV in the car park was working, so their only option was assaulting the building from the front. Leeanne had already given Verity a breakdown of the security setup in the building. Only the doors and ground-floor windows were alarmed, and there were motion sensors throughout the ground floor, which meant they'd have to get in through a first-floor window, Verity thought, as she scanned the front of the building for an obvious means of reaching the windows without the aid of a ladder. After some consideration, she walked over to the cast-iron drainpipe which ran down the left-hand corner of the building. She took a pair of pink washing-up gloves out of her pocket and pulled them on. She grasped the downpipe with both hands and gave it a vigorous tug.

'That should be fine,' she said. She then traced an imaginary line along the brickwork to the stone window ledge and nodded. 'Perfect.' She turned to Leeanne.

'Right, up you go. You'll need this,' said Verity, holding out a long screwdriver.

'You what?'

'You'll need this—to open the window.'

'What do I want to open the window for?'

'So we can get in,' said Verity, wondering if she'd missed something during their earlier conversation.

'Wouldn't it be easier to just use these?' Leeanne asked, waving a bunch of keys in front of Verity's face.

'Why didn't you say you had keys?'

'You didn't ask,' said Leeanne.

A short section of police tape, which had once run across the front of the door, had been torn and now hung from a piece of old ironwork, fluttering occasionally when the breeze caught it.

'It looks like we're not the first to be here,' said Verity, as Leeanne turned the key in the lower door lock.

Once inside, Leeanne went to the alarm control panel and

punched in the code, which had been written down on a post-it note and stuck to the side of the panel. Verity produced a small wind-up torch and began winding it furiously; the sound of the dynamo spinning now seemed deafeningly loud. After winding the torch to the point where her forearm ached and sweat had formed on her brow, Verity clicked the torch on and cursed its feeble output. She'd taken no more than six steps when she crashed into a fire extinguisher. Verity stumbled and crashed to the floor, her pathetic torch skittering away, the sickly yellow light diminishing with every rotation until it faded to black.

Overhead, old fluorescent lights flickered into life. Verity looked up at Leeanne, who had extended her arm to help her up.

Verity crept stealthily upstairs to the first floor, Leeanne close behind, unsure why her friend was moving about like a cat. Verity stopped outside the staff canteen and took the round doorknob in her gloved hand and turned it slowly, holding her breath as she did so.

'Boo!'

Verity jumped as though the door handle had been electrified, almost punching herself in the face as she crashed into Leeanne.

'Stop doing that! You scared the life out of me, you soft sod!'

Leeanne laughed and gave Verity a good-natured shove.

'There's nobody here, you know—apart from us.'

'Yes, I know that, but still…' said Verity, taking slow, measured breaths.

'You still haven't told me what it is you're hoping to find,' said Leeanne, as she dragged out a chair and sat down. Verity walked over to the kitchen area and knelt down in front of the fridge.

'I'm looking for...' She pulled open the fridge door. '... this,' she said, pointing at the shelf at the bottom of the fridge door.

'What am I supposed to be looking at?'

'Bloody hell! Where is it?' Verity began pulling things out of the fridge door and yanked out the salad crisper. Nothing. Then she started taking out contents of the shelves and began stacking the personalised lunchboxes next to her, their contents sweaty and beginning to turn.

Leeanne watched her. 'I can't help but think that as midnight snacks go, this one is pretty grim. I would have ordered pizza if I'd known you were this desperate. What are you looking for?'

Verity crouched on her haunches and peered into the gloomy interior of the fridge, in case it had been shoved into the back. Again, nothing.

'There was a bag of syringes in here,' said Verity, standing up. 'Whoever it was that broke the police tape must have taken them. Bugger and balls!' Verity kicked the side of the fridge, hard enough to shift it a few inches, revealing an unpleasant corner of grime, mouldy food, and furry cutlery on the floor.

'Never mind, at least we tried,' said Leeanne, rubbing Verity's back.

Verity's head jerked upright. 'What am I saying? This is fantastic!'

'What is?'

'The syringes. If someone has broken in here just for those, then they must be significant,' said Verity, as she feverishly began throwing the lunchboxes back onto the shelves. 'If we can find the syringes, we've found our murderer.'

'Hang on. So now you think it is murder?'

'It certainly seems that way,' said Verity, as she tossed the last remaining items into the fetid fridge.

Verity's heavy-handedness caused a frosted white light cover to fall out of the fridge. Verity sighed and picked it up, dropping onto her knees to reattach it. It was then that she saw the small black box dangling from a piece of black tape.

'What the hell is that?' She tugged at the tape, freeing the small black box.

They peered at it curiously. Verity wasn't great with technology, but it was obvious even to her that this was a spy camera.

'It looks like somebody was really getting fed up with people eating their sarnies,' Leeanne said, picking up the camera and examining it.

'It does, doesn't it?' Verity said, considering the wider implications of this discovery.

'The question is, how do we get inside it?'

18

A short time later, the two women were in Verity's office. A quick internet search revealed that the camera was a high-end model, which had both Wi-Fi and an external memory card.

Upon seeing the price of the camera, Leeanne gave a low whistle. 'Whoever set this camera up was pretty serious about catching the sandwich thief,' she said, as she ejected the memory card, and inserted it into a hitherto undiscovered slot in the side of Verity's laptop. Leeanne took command of the computer, and after a few keystrokes, a grid of video stills began to populate the screen. Leeanne scrolled through the list and clicked on a few videos at random. The video quality was surprisingly good, given the tiny size of the device, and each of the videos was time-stamped. The image was distorted by the fisheye lens, but it was certainly good enough that you could make out the different lunchboxes and the hands going in and out—there was Karina, with her fat-free yoghurts, there was Brian, depositing a substantial pork pie. Then there were Verity's own hands, as she reached in to get the milk a few days ago. There was even audio on the video, though it mostly picked up the internal humming and gurgling of the fridge.

The video which interested Verity most of all was the last one on the list. The one with yesterday's date on it.

'Play that one.'

In two clicks, the video was playing full screen. Fading in from black, the video came into focus as the tiny lens adjusted to the light. It showed the contents of the fridge and the outside world, to a distance of about three feet. It was difficult to work out what they were looking at, at first, but after a few seconds, it became apparent that it was a denim-clad leg. Seconds later, the figure knelt, and an arm came into shot. The camera picked up some sound—the rattling of shelves, the hum of the compressor, a soft groan—a man's voice? A hand reached in. There was a flash of something indistinct—a bag, perhaps? The leg again. The fridge door closing. Fade to black. The sound of the fridge humming for a few seconds in the darkness, until the camera stopped recording. Seeing this, Verity knew she was onto something. The event itself was significant, but the timing removed all doubt from her mind. This was it.

'Rewind that,' said Verity, pacing the office as she considered what it meant.

Leeanne dutifully replayed the video.

'Who is that?'

'It looks like a man, I'd say,' said Leeanne.

'I think so. See if you can stop it and get a clear shot of the hand.'

Leeanne clicked on the video to bring up the controls and moved the cursor over the pause button, her finger poised over the touchpad. The hand appeared. Click. It was blurry and indistinct. Click, click. The video advanced a few frames. A man's hand. Another click. There! Click.

Now a hand appeared suspended in time. The fingers were clear. Definitely a man's hand. The nails were clipped, and on the wrist, a flash of gold from a wristwatch. A pinky ring, also gold. Very ornate. Very distinctive.

The women spoke in unison. 'Tony!'

They continued through the rest of the video, frame by frame, until Verity was able to confirm that the item Tony was removing from the fridge was the bag she'd seen when she was getting the milk out of the fridge on the afternoon of her interview, which contained some syringes and a blue plastic box, about the size of a matchbox. If there was any writing indicating the nature of the contents, it wasn't visible, and she couldn't recall seeing any at the time.

'What do you think's in that bag?' asked Leeanne.

'I'm not sure. Drugs of some description, I'd say, by the looks of it.'

A look of realisation spread across Leeanne's face.

'Oh. My. Actual. Gee,' she said, her hand coming up to cover her mouth.

'You think Tony's drugged Carl, don't you?'

'It would explain Carl's unusual behaviour just before he died, wouldn't it?'

Leeanne nodded slowly, her eyes wide as she mulled this over. It was hard to imagine Tony was a murderer. But it was hard to imagine that any of them were capable of murder.

'But what if we're wrong? What if it's just his medicine or something?' said Leeanne.

'Of course we could be wrong,' said Verity. 'Does Tony have any serious medical conditions that you're aware of?'

Leeanne shook her head.

'And it if was some important medication,' Verity said, 'He could have just asked the police to get it for him, surely, or get more from his GP.'

'I suppose so,' said Leeanne. 'But why would he want to kill Carl? Because of the money he owed him, do you think?'

'It could be. I don't know. But what I do know is that Tony was keen enough to get rid of that bag that he broke through police tape the minute the police had left the place. If it was some vital medication, he wouldn't have a problem getting some more without needing to break into a potential crime scene.'

'So now what do we do?'

Verity's answer surprised herself as much as it did Leeanne.

'We have to take this to the police.'

If this didn't convince them, Verity reasoned, then nothing would.

19

'Are you sure you want to do this?' Leeanne asked as she parked her car outside Brenton police station. After a sleepless night mulling this over, Verity had made her mind up.

'I don't want to, but I think it's the right thing to do,' Verity said as she got out of the car.

'Okay then. Call me when you're done, and I'll come and pick you up.'

Verity gave her a half-hearted smile. 'Thanks.' Leeanne drove off, giving a short beep and a wave as she exited the car park. Verity watched her go, thinking vaguely about what a good friend she'd found in Leeanne. After a short internal battle, she headed for the entrance to the police station, and said a little prayer to a god she didn't really believe in, on the off chance he believed in her.

The reception area was a single window in the centre of a wall of black panelling which ran from floor to ceiling, similar to those found in a bank. The only colour on the walls came from a cork board covered in posters which addressed such cheery topics as people trafficking, drugs, scams, confidential crime hotlines, and suicide prevention. Opposite the counter was a row of four blue and chrome chairs. The only occupant of the chairs was a man of pensionable age with a bad leg and a perpetual phlegmy cough. Verity hoped she wouldn't be kept waiting for long. She walked up to the vacant counter and pressed a button marked "Please ring for attention". Somewhere behind the counter, an angry buzzer sounded. A note had been taped next to the bell which read, "Please don't ring the bell repeatedly. We heard you the first time. Thank you". Below that, an addendum, written in a different hand, "Patience is a virtue". Someone—presumably a visitor—had added their own message beneath this, "No she bloody isn't, ask Dave! LOL".

The man coughed wetly into his sleeve before sniffing loudly and swallowing. Verity gagged. Her finger was hovering over the button again when a bulldog of a receptionist appeared at the window, giving Verity a disapproving glare. *Don't you dare.*

Verity withdrew her finger and felt her cheeks grow warmer.

The receptionist pressed a button on the intercom, and speakers on Verity's side of the counter came to life. 'How can I help you?'

'I need to speak to a detective, please. Detective Hodge or Yates. Preferably the latter,' she said.

'Can I ask what this is regarding?'

'It's about an ongoing investigation. I've got some information that might help them.'

'Can I take your name, please?' the receptionist asked, inputting Verity's answers into a computer.

'Yes, it's Meadows. Verity Meadows. The detectives know who I am.'

'Very well. If you take a seat over there,' she said, pointing to the only available seats, 'Someone will come through to speak to you in a few minutes.'

The man with the syrupy cough looked up and gave Verity a smile, revealing the sum total of three tobacco-stained teeth. He patted the chair next to him. 'Sit down, love. Dunna worry, I don't bite,' he said.

Given the number of teeth left in his head, this was stating the bleeding obvious, Verity thought.

Reluctantly, she sat on the seat furthest from him and smiled politely, holding her handbag across her lap defensively.

'Y'anna got any fags, 'ave yer? I'm fair gasping.'

From nowhere, a tinny electric voice said, 'No smoking!'

The man stuck out his bottom jaw. 'Miserable buggers.'

A short time later there was a beep, and a dooropened. Detectives Hodge and Yates walked through it. Seeing the look of immense satisfaction on Hodge's face immediately made Verity regret her decision.

'As I live and breathe, look who it is, Yates—Mrs Meadows. We were just talking about you, weren't we, Yates?'

Verity thought he was only one "Cor blimey" away from going full Dick Van Dyke.

'Indeed,' said Yates flatly, acknowledging Verity without any of the theatrics.

Verity stood up and found herself torn between talking and fleeing.

'I have some information about your investigation that you might find useful.'

'Well, you'd better come through and tell us all about it, hadn't you,' said Hodge, as Yates held her key fob against an access panel and opened the door.

Verity followed them through into the space beyond, the door closing behind her with a definite click, cutting her off from freedom and all the things she loved in the world. As they moved deeper into the bowels of the building, a couple of lines from a poem she'd loved as a child came to her.

> 'Will you walk into my parlour?' said the Spider to the Fly,
>   ''Tis the prettiest little parlour that ever you did spy.'

20

Verity was taken to Interview Room 2, where she was shown to her seat by Yates, who took up a seat on the opposite side of the desk alongside Hodge. Yates clicked a white switch on the wall next to the desk, which turned on the red "occupied" light above the door. She then sat down and unzipped a black leather conference folder and clicked her pen, ready to take notes. Hodge removed his suit jacket and placed it on the back of his chair, before sitting down and pushing up his sleeve garters. The room was small and functional, but Verity suddenly felt lost in this white, windowless space. A 24-hour clock hung on the wall above the table, the second hand sweeping silently across its face.

'Okay, shall we begin?'

Verity felt her gut twist.

'This all seems rather formal?'

Hodge frowned.

'Of course. You've come to us with new information relating to a serious ongoing investigation,' he said. 'What were you expecting?'

'I don't know, just a quick chat somewhere,' said Verity.

'Well, depending on what you're going to tell us, this could be a very quick chat,' said Hodge cheerily. This soothed Verity's nerves no end.

'Actually, would you like a drink before we start? A tea or coffee, perhaps?' Hodge asked. 'I think we could even stretch to a bottle of fizzy pop.'

He was smiling again.

'I'm fine, thank you.'

'Okay, but I could use a drink, if you don't mind?' He turned to Yates. 'Could you grab us a couple of bottles of water and get me a tea, please—a fresh one, not out of the machine, and make sure you let it infuse properly, I want it strong enough that I can stand a spoon up in it.' Yates had been on perpetual brew duty since she'd been assigned to him. If the police thing didn't work out, she would make a good barista by the time her training had finished. As Yates was leaving the interview room, Hodge added, 'Don't rush back.'

As the door clicked behind the trainee detective, Hodge settled back into his chair and gave Verity a predatory smile.

'It's funny how fate keeps bringing us together like this, isn't it?'

Verity felt all the warmth in the room evaporate in an instant.

'You think? I haven't laughed once,' said Verity, turning to the clock, willing the second hand to speed up.

'No, that's not true.'

Verity didn't take the bait, but Hodge continued. 'I have a very distinct memory of you laughing when we were in the supermarket.'

The supermarket.

'Oh, for God's sake, man, are you still going on about that?'

165

'It's Detective Hodge to you, and yes, I am still going on about that.'

This man was clearly out to make her life utterly miserable, for no other reason than he had taken a personal dislike to her and was using his position as police officer to justify it, and Verity had just about had enough of it, and she made her feelings known.

'Detective? What a joke. You couldn't detect your backside with both hands if someone gave you directions,' she said, watching his smile fade.

'I see. Like that, is it?'

'Yes, Hodge, I think it is,' said Verity, finding it harder to disrespect the detective for the second time in as many seconds. Verity was far from perfect, but she'd been brought up properly, and a big part of that had been respecting her "elders and betters", and though Verity wasn't sure Hodge was either of those things, his occupation should command some respect.

'You're not the first person to underestimate me, Meadows, and you won't be the last,' said Hodge, his smile returning, much to Verity's consternation.

'That doesn't surprise me,' she said haughtily.

'Really? Well, here's something else that might surprise you. I did manage to detect something all on my own.'

'Congratulations. I hope they gave you a gold star,' said Verity uneasily, feeling the momentum shift back in the detective's favour.

How long does it take to make a cup of bloody tea? she thought, willing Yates to return.

'Let me tell you what I detected, Mrs Meadows, or should I say... Mrs Palmer?'

Verity reeled from this gut punch. It was the first time she'd heard anyone say her married name in months. If the detective knew she was using her maiden name, she knew there was worse to come.

'And guess what else I detected? I detected that your husband is currently holidaying in Clebe.'

Verity's skin crawled at the mention of the place. She shifted uncomfortably in her seat.

In contrast, Hodge was relishing the moment.

'He's slumming it a bit, though, isn't he? HMP Clebe. Have you seen the TripAdvisor ratings for that place? Shocking.'

Verity tensed, waiting for the follow-up blows, and Hodge duly delivered them.

'Eighteen months for fraud, eh? It must be very difficult for you, alone in a strange place, with all this going on?'

'He's innocent!' Verity said, her cheeks glistening with tears.

'Aren't they all.'

'Obviously not, no, but he is.'

'Really? So innocent that you have to change your name and move halfway across the country to hide your dirty little secret from everyone?'

'It is not a "dirty little secret", but it certainly isn't something you choose to broadcast—as soon as anyone gets a whiff of it, you're damned. You have no idea what it's been like. We've lost our business, our money, friends, everything—gone overnight!'

'And your husband tried to disappear, too, didn't he?'

Verity slammed her hand against the desk. 'No! I'm not going through this again—and why are we even discussing this, anyway? Roger was set up by Pickering. And if the police bothered to follow the paper trail, they'd find him—and our money—and my husband would be home, where he belongs, not rotting in that godforsaken hole!'

There was a beep, and the door opened. Hodge watched as

Yates struggled with the door and a tray of drinks. She saw that Verity was crying. 'Have you, err?'

'Yes, she knows we know, so let's get on with it, shall we?'

Yates took her cue and resumed the interview.

'What is it you'd like to tell us, Mrs Palmer?'

Verity looked like the stuffing had been ripped out of her, as she had almost folded in on herself.

'Verity, please,' said Verity, before blowing her nose violently into a tissue.

'No problem.'

Verity took a big breath in and exhaled steadily before speaking. 'Nothing. I was mistaken,' she said, suddenly so acutely aware of the USB memory stick in her handbag, that it almost felt as though it was calling out to her. She was damned if she was going to go out of her way to help Hodge now. *Damn him and damn the consequences.*

'Nothing?' said Yates.

'That's right. I thought I'd remembered something he'd said when he burst into the interview, but I can't remember what it was—or even if he'd actually said it. Sorry.'

Hodge took over. 'So let me get this straight. You—the wife of a man who has been convicted of fraud—'

'Wrongly convicted,' said Verity, talking over him.

'—convicted of fraud, who is a key witness in what might turn out to be the murder of a man who was known to have financial problems—a man you were seen getting into a heated argument with, mere moments before his death—has come to us to tell us that you have information about the case, but upon discovering that we know about your husband's unfortunate predicament, you've conveniently forgotten what it was you were going to tell us?'

Verity, who had no fight left in her now, just nodded.

'And you expect us to believe that?'

'You'll believe what you want, Detective. The alternative would be for you to go out there and investigate something, and I don't think that's going to happen any time soon.'

'You can see how that looks to us, can't you?' said Yates.

They were interrupted by a knock on the door, and Verity was thankful for it. Yates closed her pad and went over to the door, peering out through the spyhole. It was the station commander, DI Ward. Whatever it was, it must have been serious. The running joke was that Ward would only leave his office if the building was on fire, and only then if he could be confident that he wouldn't encounter any actual police work as he made his way out of the station.

Yates opened the door and stood back, allowing Ward into the room. He didn't enter. Instead, he addressed Hodge from the threshold.

'Have you two got a minute?'

Hodge's face communicated his displeasure at being interrupted.

'Can it wait until we're done, boss?'

'No, it can't.'

Yates followed the DI out of the room. Hodge got up and rattled his chair under the desk noisily.

'Don't go anywhere,' he said, closing the door on Verity.

Hodge and Yates returned twenty-five minutes later. Hodge looked like the cat who'd got the cream.

Verity stood up as they entered. 'You took your time. I'd like to go home now, please?'

'I see. Have plans, do we?' asked Hodge.

'Yes, as a matter of fact I do,' Verity replied.

'Well, if I were you, I'd cancel them,' said Hodge, making no attempt to hide his satisfaction.

'I beg your pardon?'

Hodge ignored her and looked at the wall clock. 'Verity

Palmer née Meadows. Given new information that has just come to light, at 10.55 a.m., I am arresting you on suspicion of murder. You do not have to say anything, but it may harm your defence if you do not mention when questioned something which you later rely on in court. Anything you do say may be given in evidence.'

Her ears began to whistle, and the room seemed to expand and contract. She slumped into her seat. 'Murder? How many times do I need to tell you, I didn't murder Carl Donahue!'

'I'm not talking about Donahue, Mrs Palmer. I'm talking about Naomi Wilson.'

Verity spent the next few hours sitting in her cell in a complete daze, waiting for the duty solicitor to arrive, and thinking about poor Naomi. For lunch she'd had been given a limp cheese sandwich, a packet of crushed crisps, and a luke-warm coffee, which she'd eaten, unenthusiastically, perched on the end of a blue vinyl mattress in her pine-scented cell.

She tried in vain to process what was happening to her, before giving up and falling back onto her mattress and staring at the ceiling until her eyes began to sting.

The duty solicitor arrived later that afternoon, and Verity was taken to a private room to consult with him. Her first impressions of the man were not good. She could see he was a habitual pen chewer with a serious perspiration problem, and every few minutes he would pause mid-sentence to stifle an oniony belch. He had a reassuring manner, however, and talked her through the process, and answered her questions clearly. He then asked her to walk him through the events of that night, step by step, in as much details as possible, as he made shorthand notes. He was particularly keen to "nail down the timeline", looking for any verifiable, time-stamped details such as phone calls, witnesses who could vouch for her whereabouts, any movements which were likely to have been captured on CCTV at the time the murder took place. He drew a timeline on his pad, written neatly, for his client's benefit:

5:50PM—6:10PM (approx.): HOME. DCs Hodge & Yates visit.
6:45PM: Drives to NW HOUSE.
6:55PM: Arrives NW HOUSE.
7:20PM: Leaves NW's HOUSE. NW Alive.
7:30PM: Arrives HOME.
8:43PM: Calls LK.
9:45PM: Drives COUNCIL OFFICES.
9:55PM: Arrives COUNCIL OFFICES.
10:00PM: Meets LK. Enters COUNCIL OFFICES.
10:30PM: Leaves COUNCIL OFFICES with LK
10:40PM: Arrives HOME with LK
11:20PM (approx.): LK leaves.
11:35PM: HOME. Sleep.

The solicitor asked Verity to check and confirm this time-line was correct to the best of her knowledge. She read through it and checked her phone to confirm the exact time she'd called Leeanne, and was about to confirm that every-thing was in order when they were interrupted by the custody sergeant, a swarthy, middle-aged man, who made Verity think of a Greek pirate. The solicitor stepped out of the room to speak with the police officer, returning a moment later.

'Good news. You're going to be de-arrested, and then you'll be free to go.'

'De-arrested?' Verity had never heard the term before. 'What's changed?'

'Never underestimate the benefit of a nosy neighbour,' he said, as he packed away paperwork into his briefcase.

'I don't understand. What have my neighbours got to do with anything?'

'Not your neighbours—Naomi's. Miss Wilson was seen alive by the woman next door, who was waiting on the doorstep for her takeaway delivery driver. Her app shows it was dropped off at 7:47 p.m.—two minutes late, she says—and she's told officers that she saw Naomi at the front window.'

'Okay, but how does that prove anything? They don't know any of the stuff we've just been over, do they?'

'Presumably not.'

'I can't prove that I was somewhere else at that time yet, can I?'

'You don't need to,' the solicitor said, snapping his brief-case shut. 'One of the detectives watched you drive away from the property twenty minutes earlier.'

'What? They were following me? That bloody man! Are they allowed to do that?'

'Follow you? Yes. And you should thank your lucky stars that they were, as it proves you weren't the last person to see her alive.'

Ten minutes later, Verity had been de-arrested and was sitting on a stout stone wall in front of the police station, waiting for a taxi to collect her. She would have phoned Leeanne, but she couldn't face her at the moment. She'd hated lying to Leeanne about this, and she was worried that when she told her the truth, she'd lose her as a friend. Come what may, she couldn't continue to lie to her. But there was something she needed to take care of first.

21

HMP Clebe was a category C prison that had been built in the late eighties. The Visitor Centre had very similar decor to the police station, which was practical and uninspiring—hard-wearing blue/grey carpeting, magnolia walls. Sets of blue fabric chairs sat on either side of a low blue table, which had a dividing partition down the middle, with two chairs per side. A sharp-eyed prison officer with flame red hair sat at a desk, ever vigilant, his back against the wall, one hand cupping the other, his head moving from side to side like a human CCTV camera. Another officer walked between the desks, always making his presence known. Verity had surrendered her personal effects in another room, before reporting to the reception desk in this room, where she showed another prison officer her identification, and gave her details. There had been an awkward moment when she'd given her surname as Meadows, only to hastily correct herself. The female prison officer regarded her with suspicion, and scrutinised Verity's driving licence, looking from the black-and-white photo on the licence to the woman who stood before her. Verity whispered to her that Meadows was her maiden name. The prison officer seemed to understand and handed back the driving licence.

A list was consulted and ticked, and Verity was allowed to proceed. Roger was waiting for her at one of the tables. When she saw him, she had to look at the floor, fearing she might burst into tears. He had the beginnings of a beard now, and it was apparent that he'd lost more weight, which was something he'd been trying to do for years, without success.

As Verity approached her husband, a prison officer crossed her path. She smiled at him nervously and said hello. He nodded and continued to patrol.

'Hello, love,' Roger said, standing up to greet her, and for a moment, they stood and appraised each other.

'Hi. How are you?' she asked, fighting the urge to take him in her arms and never let him go.

'I'm holding up. Sit down.'

They sat, and as much as Verity wanted to blurt out everything that had happened to her recently, she couldn't do anything other than look at him. He wore a blue bib and some kind of electronic tag in a yellow armband over a grey sweater, with matching jogging pants and plain white trainers.

'You can talk, you know.'

'Yes, sorry. It's just hard—seeing you in here.'

The first few moments of their conversation were mostly Verity asking her husband questions about his wellbeing: are you managing to sleep, are you eating properly, are you being targeted by bullies, and so on. She stopped when Roger told her she sounded like his mother, a stinging insult in Verity's book.

Roger asked how she was, and Verity chose to give him a very sanitised version of events, reasoning that he was not in a position to change anything and that he had enough on his own plate without sharing her troubles.

Despite the fact that they only spoke briefly on the phone —either during his allotted phone time, or when he managed to snatch a few minutes of conversation with her on the smuggled mobile phone he'd bought from the unofficial prison shop—and for one hour during her fortnightly visits, finding something to talk about was surprisingly difficult.

After another round of formalities, this time about the house and the car, the conversation stalled again, so Verity took the opportunity to share what was playing on her mind.

'There's been a development at home,' she said, vaguely.

'What do you mean?'

'I've had another chat with the police this morning—'

'Bloody hell. What about now? They're not still on your back about this bloody Donahue bloke, are they?'

Roger had been following the story in the newspapers with considerable interest. Fellow inmates—or "residents" as they were known—many of whom were acquainted with Hodge in an official capacity, had reassured Roger that his wife had nothing to worry about, as Hodge wasn't quite the copper he thought he was. Being a careful man, Roger delicately pointed out that they were having this conversation in prison as they ate food from a plastic tray with plastic cutlery.

'No, it's about something else—a murder.'

Roger stood. "Murd—'

Before he could finish the word, the patrolling prison officer was at his side.

'That'll do, Palmer. Sit down,' he said sternly.

Roger sat down and composed himself, waiting for the guard to move on before he continued, his voice lowered. 'What about it? Who's been murdered?'

'A girl from the office—Naomi.'

Roger looked relieved.

'Okay. But why are they speaking to you about this?'

'Because I'd been to see her, just before she was murdered.'

'You're joking?'

'I wish. Anyway, it's fine now. A witness has given a statement to the police, and it proves I wasn't the last person to see her alive.'

'Bloody hell, Vee. What a mess.'

'Yes, it is a bit, isn't it? But there's something else—the police know about you, and about the whole name thing. I'm sorry.'

Roger closed his eyes and fumed silently for a time. 'Sorry? Why the hell would you tell them that?'

'I didn't tell them anything! He's obviously been doing some background checks on me as part of this Donahue case. It was inevitable, really.'

Roger conceded and slowly began to decompress.

'I suppose it was. He'd better not start running off at the mouth, or I'll… be less than impressed with him. We can't go through this again—I'm getting out in…' He did some mental arithmetic, 'one hundred and nineteen days, if I stay on my best behaviour.'

Verity considered the number. Almost four months. When they were together, four months could pass in a flash; without him at home, and without their old routines, four months would feel like an eternity.

The remainder of their time together passed quickly. The prison officer at the desk announced that visiting time was over. Unable to hug or kiss, the two had to make do with an exchange of blown kisses.

As the other visitors started to file out of the room, and the residents returned to their cells, Verity lingered, gazing fondly at her husband.

'I love you,' she said.

He smiled. 'I know.'

She wanted him to say it back, but she knew he wouldn't—not in public, and certainly not in front of other men, but she so desperately wanted to hear him say it. She smiled at him and turned away, not wanting him to see her crying again.

As she neared the door, he called after her.

'Vee?'

She looked at him hopefully.

'Yes?'

'Promise me you won't get into any more trouble. I'm buggered if we both end up inside.'

Swallowing her disappointment, Verity nodded and walked away, knowing that this was a promise she might not be able to keep.

22

When Verity returned from visiting her husband in prison, she immediately threw her clothes in the wash, and took a quick shower before taking a long soak in a bath so hot it made her skin itch.

Then she phoned Leeanne and apologised for not calling her after she'd finished at the police station and said they should meet at the Pig & Pickle later that afternoon, where she would explain everything. She had a hard time getting Leeanne off the phone, as she was desperate to talk about Naomi's death, which was now public knowledge, and only managed to do so by telling her that she desperately needed the loo.

Both women arrived early, and after Verity had received a most welcome hug from Leeanne, they took care of the first order of business: cocktails, with Verity opting to start with a Tom Collins, and Leeanne a Singapore Sling.

By the time they'd moved from the bar to a discreetly positioned table, Verity had taken off the top third of her drink.

Leeanne's bottom had barely touched the seat when she began speed-talking. 'I can't believe it, can you? About Naomi. Dead. It's mad, isn't it? There she was, one minute, alive, and there she was the next minute, dead! What do you think happened to her, because I think it's probably *you know what*, and I'm not the only one thinking it either, because Sue, who works with Ken who used to work at the hardware shop with Gary, said that her fella thinks it's *you know what*, too, and he should know, what with his mum being a nurse.' When she'd finally finished unspooling, Leeanne took a breath and a drink.

Verity took a moment to reassemble Leeanne's words into coherent sentences before replying.

'Well, between you, me and the gatepost,' said Verity out of the side of her mouth, 'it was *you know what*.'

Leeanne made a big O with her mouth and blinked slowly for such a long time that Verity wondered if she was rebooting.

'Oh. My. Actual! How do you know?'

'Because yesterday I was arrested on suspicion of being the person who did it.'

'Noooo,' said Leeanne, clamping her mouth between her palms. 'No way!'

'Yes way.'

'But you must have been with me when it happened? So it can't be you.'

'I know it isn't me! I think I'd know if I'd done it! And I'm pretty sure we wouldn't be discussing it over cocktails.'

'Good point. This was when you went to the police station to tell them about Tony?'

'Yes, but I didn't really get a chance to tell them anything about it.'

Leeanne thought about this over a couple of sips of her drink.

'So have they arrested anyone else for it?'

'Not that I know of,' said Verity, reviewing the cocktail selections on a chalkboard above the bar.

'It must be Tony, then. If he did *you know what* to *you know who*, then he must have done this too?'

'I certainly wouldn't discount him, but we can't say for certain, of course. Those videos don't prove anything—they're circumstantial at best. But there is something else.'

'What do you mean?' said Leeanne.

'I saw him last night, and it looked like he was on his way to Naomi's house.'

Leeanne gasped.

'Seriously? You need to go to the police with this.'

'I'd rather not go anywhere near that lot, if it's all the same with you.'

'I could take the videos to them?' said Leeanne.

'No. We need more than those videos. We need physical evidence.'

'Like those syringes?'

'Exactly like those syringes,' said Verity.

Verity went to the bar and ordered another round of cock-tails, thinking about how she was going to tell Leeanne the truth about her and Roger. As the cocktails were placed before her, Verity decided to order a shot of Dutch courage, which she knocked back in one, and spluttered her thanks to Chas. As she sat down, she bit the bullet.

'There's something else I need to tell you—about me, not this… whatever it is.'

Leeanne took an agonisingly long sip of her drink through a curly straw before speaking.

'What's that?'

'The thing is…' Verity felt Leeanne watching her intently, hanging on her every word.

Just say it!

'Look. What I'm trying to say is…'

Verity wasn't struggling to find the words; she was just struggling to say them. Leeanne took another long pull on her drink; Verity watched the yellow milky liquid work its way around the impossibly shaped pink straw.

'It's just that…'

Leeanne came up for air and dabbed her mouth with a napkin.

'Is it about your husband being in prison?'

Verity was taken aback.

Well, that certainly makes things easier.

'How the hell do you know about that?'

Leeanne tapped her nose and gave Verity a wink. 'I know people.'

'Evidently,' said Verity. 'So how do you know?'

'My cousin works in the prison.'

Verity already knew who it would be.

'She said you'd given the wrong name when you checked in, and she'd already heard me mention your name before now, so she called me and told me.'

'Well, it's good to know that it's already common knowledge,' said Verity testily.

'No, she won't tell anyone else. She's not a blabbermouth.'

'It didn't take long for her to tell you,' said Verity.

'Well, that's different, isn't it—she's family. And you're my friend, so I'm not about to tell anyone, am I?'

'Honestly?'

'Brownie's honour,' said Leeanne brightly, as she gave the three-fingered Brownie salute.

Verity began to sob. 'Thank you,' she said, taking Leeanne's hand and squeezing it. 'I'm so sorry. I would have told you if I could have.' She made eye contact with her companion. 'Please don't hate me.'

'Don't be so daft. I would have done the same thing.'

Verity sniffed and smiled. 'Thank you.'

'What's the story then?' asked Leeanne.

Verity gave a detailed and honest account of how she'd phoned the British police after discovering that their bank accounts had been cleaned out. After making a few phone calls, they'd learned that Pickering had left for the airport in the company of a woman half his age, who'd once appeared in a reality TV series. After some frantic brainstorming, Roger had remembered there was a place in the Dominican Republic that Pickering had mentioned a couple of times, and Roger had made a note of it, as he'd planned on taking Marcus there as a surprise for his fiftieth birthday. Concerned that the police would move too late, and mindful that there was no extradition treaty with the Dominican Republic, Roger said he would fly out and confront Pickering in person.

Reluctantly, Verity had agreed to return home on the next available flight, to assist the police, while Roger attempted to track down Pickering. Roger had booked them on to the next available flights, using a personal credit card, which had been hidden in their luggage, in case of emergencies.

Verity got a call from a detective in the Met's fraud squad, three days later, telling her that they'd made an arrest in relation to the incident. She was elated—until she heard the name of the man they'd arrested. They'd summoned her to the police station to make a statement. Verity had contacted their solicitor, who'd met her at the police station.

Detectives spent almost two hours questioning Verity, during which time they asked her questions about several bank transfers to offshore bank accounts in her husband's name. Verity had explained that no such accounts had been set up by her husband or herself, and told them, again and again, that Marcus had always taken care of all their financial dealings and had access to every bit of personal information he'd need to set up these accounts. Increasingly frustrated, she'd told them they were wasting time, and should be out looking for Pickering. It had been some small consolation when one of the officers had confirmed that they were currently trying to ascertain Pickering's whereabouts, as he was a significant witness in this case. Once detectives had finished questioning her, she'd been released, leaving their solicitor to speak with his other client, Roger. Verity had rushed home and sat by the telephone, searching through paperwork, gathering whatever useful documents she could find, and waiting on a call from their solicitor, saying that they were releasing Roger. Instead, they'd announced that they would be charging him with seven counts of fraud. Three months later, Roger was convicted on four of the seven counts and sentenced to eighteen months in prison. Verity had been in court that day. It was the only time in Verity's life that she had fainted.

Leeanne listened while she'd explained everything, holding her hand throughout.

'So that's why you changed your name?'

'Yes. It was Roger's idea. He said it would be easier for me to use my maiden name for a bit, while we straightened everything out, especially as I'd be on my own for the next few months.'

'And when is your husband due out?'

'About four months,' said Verity.

'Then what are you going to do?'

'I know what the second thing we're going to do is.'

'What's that?'

'Change our solicitors and get his conviction quashed. Then start suing people like it's going out of fashion, starting with previous solicitors.'

'And what about now?'

'Right now, drink. Later, go and speak to Tony.'

23

Verity and Leeanne left the pub after their third cocktail, and walked down the high street with the intention of visiting Tony while they were still sober enough to talk to a potential double-murderer and drunk enough not to realise that this was a terrible idea. The route took them near Naomi's house. They were surprised to find there was no police presence at the property. As they neared, curiosity got the better of the pair. Leeanne came to a stop on the footpath opposite the murdered woman's house. Emboldened by drink, she asked Verity if they should look at the place.

'I don't see any harm in it,' Verity replied. 'As long as we don't touch anything. Just keep an eye out for that neighbour of hers. We don't want her on the phone to the police the second we arrive.'

They crossed over the road and approached what would soon be known as "the house where that girl was murdered". More of the now familiar police tape had been placed around the boundary of Naomi's property, secured with wooden stakes, one of which had been knocked down, leaving the tape slack. Just outside the perimeter, a single bouquet of tulips lay on the path, a small card protruding from it. The sight of a single bunch of flowers lying in isolation struck Verity as desperately sad—perhaps more so than an entire wall of flowers would—as though it meant only one person cared that this woman was dead.

Verity looked over to the neighbouring house and was pleased to see the curtains were closed. A note had been pinned to the neighbour's door, but Verity couldn't make it out at this distance. She squinted to see if she could read what the note said, but could only make out fragments of it: *Seventy-five pounds, something... No pies, was that?*

Absentmindedly, she stepped over the police tape and took a few steps across Naomi's lawn, until she could see the sign clearly. It had been written in a variety of felt-tipped pens and biros, and it read:

Interview rates:-
Local Radio—£25. National Radio—£50.
Telly Vision—£75 plus hair and make-up.
(Free for Eamonn Holmes.)
NO Piers ****** Morgan!!!
No Fee. No Story. No Receipt.

'Good God. How awful,' said Verity. Though the neighbour's stance on interviews with Piers Morgan went some way to redeem the ghoul, she thought, as she approached Naomi's front door. Given the unusual layout of Badgers Rise, these two properties were the only ones to face the road, which meant that this must be the neighbour who was the last person to see Naomi alive.

'Who lives there?' Verity asked.

'That'll be Maureen Spinnaker. Right nosy cow, she is—

even nosier than me,' said Leeanne.

'Impossible,' said Verity, with a sly grin.

Like the neighbouring house, all the curtains were closed in Naomi's house. The glass panel in the front door was frosted, but there was a small square window to the side of the door that offered an unobstructed view of the hallway.

Leeanne approached the window but stopped short of looking in.

'Did they say how it happened?'

'No. They didn't say much at all. All I know is that she was found in the house.'

Verity approached the window. Grey smudges of finger-print powder on the door reminded her that they might be contaminating a crime scene, but she was now a slave to her sense of curiosity. Verity had no idea what happened to a murder scene once the body was taken away, and she was beginning to have second thoughts, but something got the better of her. She stole a few brief glances through the window, her head darting back and forth like a pigeon pecking at something suspect. She withdrew and considered what she'd seen, then looked again, lingering this time, careful not to touch the glass. It looked just as it had when she'd visited. The same cream carpet—thankfully unstained—the same novelty doormat, the same little homely flourishes, the same side table.

The table looked as if it had been moved slightly, though she couldn't be sure.

Leeanne stood some distance down the path, looking about her, clutching her colourful cardigan tightly to her chest, trying to ward off an imagined chill.

'Do you think she's watching us now?'

'The neighbour?'

'No, Naomi.'

Verity joined Leeanne.

'No, I don't, but if she is, I'd like to think she knows we're trying to get her some earthly justice.'

'That's nice. She'd like that,' Leeanne said, wiping her face with the cuff of her cardigan.

A muted bang startled them. Leeanne managed not to swear, Verity did not.

They peered over at the neighbour's house and saw an elderly woman banging on the inside of the front window. She was shouting something only she could hear. Her gesturing made it clear that she was trying to get the two trespassers to move on, and quickly.

Verity acknowledged the woman and made her way down the path. Leeanne started mouthing something at the woman, her voice barely audible. Now it was Leeanne's turn to communicate via hand gestures, and she gave the woman in the window two pairs of very pronounced vees, accompanied by a long, wet raspberry.

The woman looked momentarily shocked before disappearing from the window, no doubt heading for the front door—possibly via the broom cupboard.

Verity and Naomi stepped over the police tape, careful to avoid the solitary bouquet, keen to make a clean getaway before they got into a dustup with the neighbour, when Verity stopped dead.

The flowers—of course!

'If she comes out, distract her!'

And she turned back to Naomi's front door.

Verity's instincts had been right; something was amiss with the table, but it wasn't that it had been moved—though she was fairly sure it had—it was what was missing from the top of it: the empty vase. It had been gathering dust on a side table in the hall, certainly for several weeks, possibly even longer, only to disappear at the same time Naomi had been murdered. Verity knew full well that sometimes coincidences were just that, no matter how unlikely they seemed, but she was no fan of them. Had she simply moved the vase? Possibly.

She thought of Tony and the flowers. He had been coming to see Naomi. Perhaps she'd used the vase and put the flowers in another room?

Verity dashed to the front window, hoping to find enough of a gap in the curtains that might help her locate the flowers and prove that Tony had been here. She was in luck. She peered through the gap, cupping her hand over her eyes, and pressing her face up against the glass, no longer concerned about leaving any additional evidence of her presence here. If she could find proof that Tony had visited the dead woman after Verity, and after she'd been seen alive by the woman next door, then the police would surely have enough grounds to arrest him. The sun was over the back of Naomi's house, and the light found its way through the blinds at the rear of the house in sufficient quantity that Verity could make out enough of the room to see that the flowers were not there.

There was a noise at the neighbour's front door, the sound of chains being released, and stubborn bolts being pulled back. She could hear the woman muttering away to herself, angrily. As Ms Spinnaker's front door opened, Verity disappeared round the side of the house. She could hear raised voices from the front of the house, but had no time to pay attention to what was being said. Leeanne was more than capable of holding her own.

The ruckus couldn't have come at a better time, as it presented Verity with the opportunity to go into Naomi's garden, without worrying about getting seen by the rent-a-gob next door. The flowers would be in the kitchen, not the front room, as that was the first place you took them when they came into the house—that's where you added the water, and trimmed the stems.

On the way to the back gate, she passed three waste bins. She noticed something on the floor next to the green waste bin—a flower bud. She took out a clean tissue from her pocket and lifted the bin lid. Inside, on top of a pile of warm grass cuttings, was a scattering of broken flowers. Fresh flowers, similar to the ones she'd seen Tony carrying. Damage to the stalks suggested that the flowers had been snapped in half. A corner of the green and yellow cellophane wrapping poked out of the next bin. Thinking of the potential evidence value, Verity opened the bin and took a photo of the label with her phone. Then she saw the vase—broken into a dozen pieces, thrown in on top of neatly tied bin liners. She took a photo of the vase and broken flowers before closing the bin lids quietly. And she began to connect the dots. There was clear evidence of violence here. Things looked increasingly damning for Tony.

Verity slipped out from the side of the house unnoticed, and signalled to Leeanne, who reluctantly curtailed her exchange of insults with Maureen, who was standing on her front step brandishing a rolled-up newspaper. Leeanne walked over to Verity, clearly invigorated by the verbal jousting.

'That's right, you'd better run before the police get here,' the neighbour shouted, when she thought Leeanne was at a safe distance. 'I know where you live, young lady.'

Without warning, Leeanne turned and ran back a few feet. Wide-eyed, Maureen withdrew hastily, slamming the front door behind her.

They continued on their way to Tony's, half expecting to hear the sound of approaching police sirens.

'What got you so excited back there?' asked Leeanne.

'Tony came to see Naomi after I left her.'

'How do you know?'

'When I went in to talk to her, I noticed an empty flower vase on a table in the hallway. When I looked just now, I noticed it wasn't there anymore, so I assumed she'd moved it into another room, to put flowers in it.'

'What's that got to do with Tony?' said Leeanne.

'Do you remember when I said I saw him, and I thought he was on his way to Naomi's?'

'Yes.'

They approached a wooden memorial bench on a grass verge and continued their conversation sitting down.

'Well, I tried to see where he was going, but I lost track of him, but I noticed he was carrying a bunch of flowers.'

'And?'

'I went round the back to see if she'd put the flowers in the kitchen, thinking that if the flowers were there—'

'Then Tony must have been there too!' said Leeanne triumphantly.

'That's right. Anyway, I found the flowers in the bin, along with the vase. And look—' Verity took her phone out of her bag and scrolled through the photos she'd just taken. 'Someone has snapped the flowers in half and smashed the vase.'

'Maybe she knocked the vase over by accident, so she threw the flowers in the bin, too?'

'I don't think so. Even if it was your only vase, you'd put the flowers in a jug or something, until you could get another one. And you wouldn't snap the flowers, would you?'

'No. Not unless I was angry,' said Leeanne.

'That's what I thought. And we know she was murdered just after that.'

Verity felt the weight of her words. She'd used the word

murder so much in the last few days that she'd almost become accustomed to it. This realisation pained her.

Leeanne shuffled along the bench and turned to read the brass memorial plaque:

In loving memory of Thomas Elkes
Who often sat here and wondered
What was the point of it all?
1937—2017

'Do you really think we should be going to see Tony if we're this sure he's killed two people?' Leeanne asked. 'I don't really want our names on a bench.'

'I'm afraid that if we don't, Carl and Naomi won't get justice and someone else might get killed.'

'Yes, but what if it's us that gets killed?'

'As long as he thinks we know nothing about it, he's got no reason to kill us.'

'I'm not so sure. What reason did he have to kill those two?'

'I suppose we'd better go and find out, hadn't we?'

Leeanne nodded gravely.

They sat for a moment in silence, enjoying the warmth of the sun on their faces and watching a tractor in a distant field, dust rising in its wake. The soothing sound of birds and insects around them was a reminder that life carried on, regardless.

Leeanne patted the back of her friend's hand. 'Come on, then.'

They stood up and headed toward Tony's house.

'What do you think our bench will say?' asked Leeanne.

'In memory of Verity and Leeanne. Who knew it was a stupid bloody idea but did it anyway.'

24

By the time they'd turned into Belvedere Lane, the effects of the alcohol had worn off. Verity had asked Leeanne to point out Tony's house. His car was on the driveway, so he was likely to be at home, she said, as he rarely left home without it.

Between them, they had devised a plan of sorts. Verity would speak with Tony on the pretence of wanting to find out if anyone knew anything about Naomi. If he didn't invite her in, she would ask to use the toilet, and try to keep the conversation going from there. Before going to the door, she would call Leeanne on her phone and keep the call connected, but Leeanne would put her phone on mute so as not to draw attention to Verity's phone. Once inside, Verity would casually try to look for any clues, while making regular appearances at the front window, so Leeanne could see that she was okay. In the absence of any obvious signs of violence, if Verity's phone suddenly went off and, she saw no signal from Verity, she was to call the police immediately before screaming bloody murder.

Verity made Leeanne promise not to put herself at risk,

and Leeanne did so, adding that she had her fingers crossed so it didn't count, and that she couldn't promise she wouldn't put Tony at risk of very serious harm if he touched either of them.

Surprising herself, Verity hugged Leeanne and kissed her on the cheek.

'I'm glad I met you, Leeanne, you're utterly, utterly bonkers, but you've got a heart of gold.'

Leeanne returned the hug with interest. 'Excuse me, you're about to walk into a murderer's house and you're calling me bonkers?'

'You raise a valid point. If anything happens to me, make sure I get a nice bench, and promise you'll visit me often,' said Verity.

'Now that's a promise I can keep—unless we move away, or it's raining, or I'm busy,' said Leeanne.

'I can't ask for more than that.'

Verity approached the front door, her heart practically beating out of her chest, her mouth as dry as parchment paper, and a silent prayer on her lips.

Tony's house was in the middle of a row of three detached houses. Like many of the houses in the area, it had been rendered and painted white. The neat, untarnished roof tiles and modern UPVC windows, which featured in all three properties, gave it away as a modern construction in the traditional style. A red, two-seater convertible sports car—all flowing lines and dramatic contours—was parked outside an integral garage, roof down. The garden was well-tended if a touch unimaginative, with many of the flowers grown in two long wooden troughs, with two artificial topiary balls hanging on either side of a pea green front door. Verity rang the doorbell. Inside the house, an electronic voice announced her presence at the front door. She heard someone on the stairs, and a man's voice saying, 'Who is it, Audrey?'

She saw movement through the glass.

Tony opened the door, rocking the smart-casual look once again: faded blue jeans, white collared shirt, baby blue cardigan, and brown suede loafers.

'Oh, hello,' he said, taken aback. He gave her a perfunctory smile, flashing his dazzling Hollywood dentures. It was a smile that had no doubt made many go weak at the knees over the years, but today it fell short of the mark.

'Felicity, isn't it? You came for the job interview.'

'Verity,' she said. She was well used to new acquaintances getting her name wrong. They were always confusing it with one of the other -ity names: Felicity, Trinity, Charity, and, on more than one occasion, Chastity.

'That's right, I came for the interview.'

'Sorry, I'm better with faces than names,' said Tony. 'I take it you've heard the news?'

'Yes. Awful, isn't it?' said Verity.

'Terrible. Poor thing. And so soon after Carl's accident, as well. Let's hope that bad things don't come in threes,' he said, gazing directly at her.

Verity felt her skin crawl.

'Sorry. I take it that's why you're here?'

'Yes. I hope you don't mind, but I've been worried sick since I've heard. I had to speak to someone about it.'

'Of course. Come in. Don't worry about your shoes.'

Tony went into the house, leaving Verity to close the door. Before she did, she checked to see that Leeanne was at her post. Leeanne popped up from behind some pampas grass opposite and gave a thumbs up. Reassured by her presence, Verity put the door on the latch and closed it behind her.

The house was immaculate and smelled strongly of sweet pea air freshener.

'Are you sure it's convenient? I heard you had company,' said Verity.

'Company?' he said, confused.

'I heard you talking to a woman.'

Tony opened the kitchen door and a grey French bulldog with a plush carrot in its mouth came over to investigate the visitor.

'Oh, no, that was just Audrey,' he said, picking up the dog and rubbing its belly. 'Wasn't it, Aud?'

Verity fussed over the dog as Tony held it. This was not what she'd been expecting at all. It was hard to imagine a double-murderer owning a toy bulldog named after a Hollywood icon.

The kitchen was beautiful—a modern farmhouse kitchen, clean and rustic, white gloss units, white marble, raw oak, and copper accents throughout.

'This is rather lovely,' said Verity, admiring the room and looking for anything out of the ordinary.

'It should be; it cost a small fortune. Take a seat,' he said, putting Audrey down and hoisting himself up onto a bar stool.

'Actually, I'll stand if you don't mind. My back's been bothering me for a few days,' she said, gravitating toward the front window.

'What have you heard then?'

'Not much, really. I heard some people talking about it in the shop this morning, saying that Naomi had been found dead. I wasn't even sure that they meant the same person until one of them said she worked at the parish council. I couldn't believe it. What about you?'

'Well,' he said, lowering his voice, 'It's all over the internet that she was murdered.'

'Murdered?' said Verity, doing a good job of feigning surprise.

'That's what they're saying,' he said, getting up from his stool.

'Coffee?' He fired up a behemoth of a coffee machine.

'Yes, please. Go on,' said Verity, hoping that this would be where he came undone.

'The postman told me one of his colleagues found her this morning, lying at the bottom of the stairs,' he said, over the noise of the machine grinding coffee beans. 'So, I went online to check if it was true, and it's all over Facebook.'

This was some performance, Verity thought. If the prison put on a Christmas pantomime, Tony should get the lead role.

'Someone in the comments, whose mum works as a cleaner at the police station, said that they'd arrested a sixty-year-old woman on suspicion of murdering her.'

'Sixty? The chee—gee whiz! Really?' she said, trying to mask her indignation.

'I know, right? Apparently, she's rough as houses, too,' said Tony, as he filled two mugs with coffee.

'Well, don't believe everything you read on the internet,' said Verity.

'I know that, but there's got to be some truth to it, hasn't there? I mean, everyone's saying it.'

She had to hand it to Tony; his performance was Oscar-worthy. Maybe that's how some murderers got away with it for so long, believing their own lies. It was time to see if she could get him to slip up.

'But I don't understand why someone would want to murder Naomi. How could you do something like that?'

Tony appeared to be considering his response.

'There are plenty of good motives for murder: lust, love, greed, and good old-fashioned revenge.'

'Which one do you think this is?' she asked.

'I don't know—a jealous boyfriend, I expect. She was a pretty thing.' He pulled open the fridge door.

'Milk and sugar?'

And there, in the door, next to the milk, was the very same bag of syringes Verity had seen previously.

Got you.

'No thanks.'

You're not bumping me off that easily, you murderous bastard!

'Has anyone said how she died?' Verity asked, hoping that her nerves would hold just a little while longer.

'No. I don't suppose anyone knows yet.'

'That's not strictly true, is it?'

'Isn't it?'

'No, it isn't.'

Tony thought about this. 'Well, I suppose the police must know, or they wouldn't be able to charge someone with murder.'

'That's right,' said Verity. 'And I tell you who else would know.'

'Who?' said Tony, taking a drink of his coffee.

'You!'

Tony spluttered, spraying coffee over the pristine worktops.

'What?'

'You heard me! You poisoned Carl and then you murdered Naomi.'

'What? Where the hell did you get that idea from?'

'It's more than an idea, Tony. I've got evidence. Evidence that you poisoned Carl and visited Naomi the night she was murdered.'

'Wow, that's some story,' Tony said, as he pulled off a few sheets of kitchen roll from a nearby dispenser and wiped coffee from the granite worktops.

'Isn't it just?'

Tony gave a hollow laugh. 'So, you think I've murdered two people and yet here you are, standing in my kitchen, alone? You really didn't think this through, did you?'

Verity suddenly felt quite vulnerable, but didn't show it. 'Who says I'm on my own?' she said, holding up her phone to show him it was active. 'There's a strike team standing by, and they're just waiting on my word.'

'And by "strike team" you mean Leeanne Keating, presumably?'

'Not necessarily,' said Verity unconvincingly.

'Well, that's what it says on your phone.'

Verity turned her phone in her hand. 'That's because she's the strike coordinator.'

'Brilliant,' Tony said, evidently amused by it all. He sat down again. 'Come on then, let's hear about this evidence of yours.'

'I'm serious,' said Verity, who was more than a bit annoyed that Tony seemed to think this was a joke.

'Oh, I don't doubt it,' said Tony. 'Let's hear it then, from the beginning.'

'Fine. With pleasure.' She cleared her throat. 'You've admitted that Carl Donahue owed you several thousand pounds—'

'Yes, I did, and yes, he does—or did, at least.'

'And you admitted that he was behind with his payments.'

'He was—by about five hundred pounds, I believe.'

Verity had assumed it was more than that, but this didn't change the facts. She continued. 'So, I put it to you that, fed up with being messed about, and having to chase him constantly for money, you poisoned him shortly before my interview, which is why you were both late.'

Tony shook his head in disbelief. 'This is great. Let me get this clear. You're saying that I poisoned Carl because he owed me money? That's what you're going with?'

'Yes.'

'That makes perfect sense, doesn't it? Because everyone knows that murdering someone is a great way to motivate them to pay off their debts.'

'I've got evidence, remember?'

'Oh yes, silly me. I forgot about the "evidence". So how did I do it then?'

'You did it with whatever poison is in those syringes in your fridge. The very same syringes that you broke into the office on Sunday night for, to stop the police finding them.'

Tony's expression changed to one of surprise. 'How the hell do you know that?'

'I told you, evidence.' After a painfully long time, Verity eventually managed to bring up the video footage of Tony on her phone, careful not to disconnect the call to Leeanne.

She played the video for him, holding the phone sideways, but maintaining a safe distance. Tony watched the video clip closely, squinting as he tried to make sense of the footage. 'Is that inside the fridge?'

Verity nodded as the video clip ended.

'Why the hell is there a camera in the fridge?'

'Because someone was taking other people's food, and someone had clearly had enough of it.'

'Of course,' said Tony.

'But it ended up catching a murderer and not a thief,' said Verity.

Tony swivelled on his stool, opened the fridge, took out the bag in question, and shook it.

'You think I poisoned Carl with this stuff?'

'That's right.'

'I poisoned him with tooth whitener?'

Verity felt the beginnings of doubt creeping in, but pressed on. 'You say it's tooth whitener, but it could be anything. And who in their right mind breaks into an active crime scene, late at night, for a bag of tooth whitener?'

'Well, you've got me there,' said Tony. 'Apart from a few minor points. Like the fact that I didn't break in because I have a key, and it wasn't an active crime scene because the police had already told me they had finished there, and the fact that it really is just tooth whitener, which I'd picked up that morning from my dentist. You can ask them if you like.'

'But that doesn't make sense,' said Verity, doubt now starting to pour in like seawater into the hull of a stricken ship. 'He must have been poisoned. We all saw how he was behaving. And why would you suddenly need teeth whitening stuff at that time of night?'

'Because sometimes people act strangely, and because I wanted to whiten my teeth for a date the next day, and I didn't have any at home.'

Verity sat on the window ledge and gathered her thoughts.

The date. He was going on a date.

'Ah, so you admit that you were going on a date then?'

Tony pulled a face at this. 'Oh, we're moving on from the poisoning now, are we? Yes, I was going on a date. I told you that a minute ago!'

'And the woman you were on a date with was found dead the next morning!'

Tony leapt up from his seat, his voice rising to meet Verity's. 'Woman? Naomi, you mean?'

'Yes! Of course I mean Naomi!'

'You think I was on a date with her?'

'I don't think it, I know it—I saw you, with the flowers, the same ones I found in her bin, just now!'

'You couldn't be more wrong if you tried, love.'

'Explain the flowers then?'

'I took her some flowers to cheer her up. So what? I can't believe she threw them in the bin though, the ungrateful cow.'

'You said it was a date.'

'No, I said I was going on a date, but it wasn't with her.'

'You did! You said she was pretty. And you admit that you took her flowers. And now you're trying to tell me you were going on a date with someone else?'

'That's exactly what I'm telling you.'

'And you expect me to believe that?'

'I don't care what you believe,' he said, fighting to regain his composure. 'You're not the police.'

'I know I'm not, but I'll be taking all this to them, don't you worry. And you don't think they'll buy your "it wasn't a date" nonsense, do you?'

Tony chewed at his thumbnail, his eyes now unfocused, lost in thought. Verity let him be. *This is it*, she thought—*a confession.*

Finally, Tony spoke. 'Yes, I was on a date, but it wasn't with Naomi.'

'Oh, really,' said Verity. 'What's the name of this mysterious woman then?'

'I can't give you a name,' said Tony.

'You mean you won't give me her name.'

'No, I can't. I promised!'

'Fancy that,' said Verity.

'It's true, I swear!'

'Come off it! Do you honestly think the police are going to believe that?' She put on a voice, '"I'm sorry, officer, I cannot reveal her name—I swore to protect her honour".'

Tony snapped, standing up so quickly that his barstool toppled over, sending Audrey skittering across the floor and into her bed. 'That's enough!'

Verity flinched, and backed away to the kitchen door, ready to make a run for it.

No sooner than he had his little outburst, his anger subsided. He righted the barstool and apologised to Verity, who looked quite shaken.

'I wasn't with a mystery woman,' said Tony, defeated.

'Who were you with then?'

'I was with a man.'

If Verity had taken a drink of her coffee, it would have been her turn to wipe it off the kitchen units.

'Oh. Oh. I see,' said Verity. 'I wasn't—I didn't know.' Tony's unexpected revelation had knocked the wind out of her sails.

'I'm not in the habit of broadcasting it, so I'd prefer you kept that to yourself.'

'Of course. That's your business, but you shouldn't have to hide who you are.'

'I'm not bothered about what people think about me, but the man I'm seeing is quite a bit younger than me, and he hasn't come out yet, because he's scared how his parents will react when he tells them. They're quite old-fashioned in that respect.'

'Ah. I see.'

Verity considered the implications of this new information. 'The fact that you're gay doesn't mean you didn't kill Naomi, and it doesn't change the fact that you were the last person to see her alive.'

'But I didn't kill her, and I wasn't the last person to her alive,' said Tony. 'But I think I know who was.'

25

Armed with fresh intelligence, Verity left Tony's house at a pace, leaving Leeanne to scramble to catch up with her. If what he'd told her just now was true, they still needed to find the proverbial smoking gun—and fast. On the other hand, if it turned out that Tony was lying, then they had more than enough evidence to pass on to the police.

From there they went directly to Verity's cottage, where they trawled through hundreds of video clips on her laptop, going back over two weeks. Leeanne was in the driving seat again, with Verity giving directions.

'Can you just bring up videos from the day of Carl's death?' Verity asked.

With a few clicks, Leeanne had reduced the list of videos to just fifteen.

'That's better,' said Verity, as she put on a dainty pair of reading glasses.

'What are we looking for now?' Leeanne asked as the first video loaded.

'I want to see if anyone tampers with Carl's lunch,' said Verity.

'Do you still think that he was drugged then, just not by Carl?'

'I think so. It's the most obvious explanation for his sudden change in behaviour.'

The first video began playing. The video showed Karina sliding her lunchbox onto the top shelf and a container of milk next to it.

'If someone did slip him something, couldn't they have put it in his drink?' said Leeanne as they watched the video. Verity made notes in the back of a seldom used daily diary, writing down Karina's name, the time and the items she placed in the fridge, and left a space to add additional comments.

They worked methodically through the videos. The first few videos, spaced a few minutes apart, showed a variety of people depositing their lunch items. By now Verity had noted the names of all those present at the time of Donahue's death, alongside a list of their lunch items, except for Tony. The next video, timestamped 9:53 a.m., showed Tony depositing the bag of syringes he said he'd picked up from his dental surgery that morning.

There were another five videos at around 11 a.m. These showed people getting milk for their drinks, and a couple of the girls taking out lunchboxes, removing a chocolate biscuit, what appeared to be a scone, and some carrot sticks and a dip. Verity had been paying close attention to Carl's lunchbox and was certain that nobody had touched it since Carl had put it in the fridge that morning.

Leeanne confirmed that this was an unofficial ten-minute tea break, which usually ran to nearer twenty minutes, depending on whether Carl was in the office that day.

The next video clip was recorded at 11:55 a.m., only a few moments after Verity had arrived at the council offices, she recalled. Leeanne clicked on the file. It showed the unmistakable doughy hand of Carl Donahue reaching into the fridge and snatching up his lunchbox. Next, he was seen returning his lunchbox and removing Karina's lunchbox. A few seconds later, the lunchbox was returned, the contents unplundered. Then he blindly grabbed at the next lunchbox along—a clear plastic box with lime green clips—Naomi's, according to Verity's notes. When the lunchbox was returned to the fridge, it was apparent that it was a sandwich short of a satisfying lunch.

'It looks like we've found the lunchbox bandit,' said Leeanne.

'A few days too late,' said Verity, ruefully.

The final video was captured shortly after midday, and it showed Verity trying to find the milk. The audio on the video was thin and choppy, but Verity recognised her own voice as she reacted to the fridge's distinctly cheesy aroma. Even now, just the act of watching the video caused Verity to wrinkle her nose.

'That's all of them,' said Leeanne. 'And nobody touches Carl's lunch.'

'Go back to the last lot of videos,' said Verity, urgency in her voice.

'Why? Nobody touches Carl's lunchbox, I'm sure of it.'

'Because it's not Carl's lunchbox we should be watching, it's Naomi's.'

The pair diligently watched each of the videos recorded during the unofficial tea break.

One video stood out, one with lots of hands diving in and out of the fridge. First, they watched it at full speed, then again at half speed. Finally, they went through it virtually frame by frame. Verity saw it first. 'There!' She pointed at the hand frozen on the screen, a barely discernible square of something on the tip of a finger, caught in the act of transferring it from one lunchbox to Naomi's.

Verity's scalp tingled as she began to understand the significance of what she was looking at. This single image was pivotal to the whole sorry affair. And all thanks to someone who'd had enough of Carl Donahue helping himself to other people's lunches.

'I don't understand. What am I looking at?'

Verity pointed at the hand on the screen, 'That, my girl, is our murderer.'

Tony answered on the second ring.

'Hi, Leeanne.'

'It's not Leeanne, it's Verity. I'm using her phone.'

'Oh, hello,' he said, sounding less than happy to hear this.

'Listen, I need your help,' said Verity.

'Okay,' said Tony cautiously. 'What do you need?'

'Can you call a meeting this evening to get everyone together? I appreciate it's a bit short notice, but it's important.'

'Why?'

'I'll explain later. Can you do it?'

Tony considered this. 'We've already got a meeting scheduled for tomorrow at four-thirty at the office to discuss coming back to work. Is that any good for you?'

'No, I don't think we can risk leaving it another day.'

Verity could hear Tony sucking his unfeasibly white teeth. 'Hmm. I could say I've got an important appointment tomorrow, so we need to bring it forward? It's cutting it a bit fine, though.'

'That sounds perfect, do it,' said Verity. 'Whatever you do, make sure everyone attends, and don't mention the murders. We don't want anyone getting spooked.'

'Murders?' he said, emphasising the plural. 'So, Carl was murdered, then?'

'It certainly looks that way,' said Verity gravely.

Tony began to ask questions, but Verity cut him off. 'I'm not getting into this now. All will become apparent later.'

'Oh, okay.'

'Tell me, do you have access to all the computers in the office?'

'Yes, why?'

'Good. Because I need to check something. Text Leeanne once everything is confirmed.'

Next, she called DC Hodge.

'Brenton CID. DC Hodge,' came the muffled voice. It sounded like she'd caught him eating lunch, and by the sounds of it, he was trying to eat it in one mouthful.

'Don't you know it's rude to speak with your mouth full?'

'It's not full,' he replied. 'Who is this and what do you want?'

'It's Mrs Meadows,' she said, making a point of emphasising her surname. 'And what I want is to give you your murderer.'

'Handing yourself in, are we, Meadows? I knew you'd buckle, eventually.'

'Your wit is second only to your table manners, Detective. Now, do you want this or not? I could pass this information on to another, less senior detective, if you'd rather not be bothered with it. I'm sure it would do their career prospects wonders.'

'Look, stop messing about and say your piece.'

'Not yet. And I have a question for you, too. I don't expect you to answer directly, but this should prove to you that what I've got to share with you is worth listening to. Okay?'

Hodge exhaled heavily, causing Verity to move the phone away from her ear.

'Whatever, just get on with it,' he said, staring at the half-eaten Cornish pasty he'd set aside.

'I assume you've had the results back from Donahue's toxicology report?'

'I'm listening,' said Hodge, his focus shifting.

Verity put on her reading glasses and quickly consulted her notes.

'It's positive for lysergic acid diethylamide, am I right? Don't ask me to spell it, and yes, I have been Googling.'

She heard a shuffling of paper and heavy breathing.

'Okay. You've got my attention, Meadows. What do you want?'

'I want you to meet me at the parish council offices at six-thirty tonight, on the dot. And for God's sake, be discreet, there can't be any sign of a police presence. Do you understand?'

'This is not my first rodeo, Meadows.'

'I know, but it might be the first one where you don't appear as the clown.'

'Who the hell do you think you're speaking to?' Verity could practically feel the heat from his enraged face emanating through the phone. 'I'll—'

'Detective? Detective. Calm down and listen to me. I need you to bring handcuffs and a large cool bag.'

26

Verity and Leeanne arrived at the parish council offices ahead of the group. They had travelled in Leeanne's car, and parked in the car park, well away from the spot beneath the now boarded-up window on the top floor. A few moments later, they heard the crunch of gravel and saw Tony's red convertible pulling up. He parked alongside them and got out of the car, peeling off a pair of gold mirrored sunglasses as if he'd just arrived at a red-carpet event, hooking the arm into the V of his pink, slim-fit shirt.

The trio made their way around to the front door, where they were joined by Hodge and Yates, who'd arrived on foot. There was a curt exchange of greetings before they went inside. Yates was carrying a folded blue bag with little dancing penguins printed on it. Verity was pleased to see that her request to bring a cool bag had been taken literally.

As they made their way upstairs, Hodge addressed Verity. 'This had better be good, Meadows, or I may be using these on you,' he said, dangling a pair of handcuffs before her.

'Oh, it will be,' Verity said confidently.

The three remaining members of staff weren't due to arrive until half past seven, which gave them just under an hour to prepare. Verity wasted no time at all and asked Tony to log in to Naomi's PC. Once they were logged in, Leeanne set to work under the watchful eye of the detectives and, in a matter of a few clicks, was able to confirm their suspicions, when Leeanne discovered a folder on Naomi's desktop which contained videos taken from the hidden camera in the fridge. Verity then left Tony with Leeanne, and led the detectives through to the staff restroom where she ran through some possible scenarios, should things not go to plan, before revealing a key piece of evidence to them. She did not, however, reveal any information about the identity of the murderer, much to Hodge's irritation, promising that all would become apparent. Hodge had pointed out that she was obstructing justice, but Verity stood firm on the matter, and told him to put a sock in it when he persisted. Through no fault of her own, Verity had been subjected to one of the most traumatic experiences of her life, and she believed that she needed this to bring the whole nasty affair to an end, to give her closure. And if she were to lift this cloud of suspicion that hung over her, then what better way to do so than in front of a room full of witnesses? Verity knew the story would soon get around the village and hoped this meant that the locals might finally stop giving her sideways glances and whispering behind her back.

Once they were done, the two detectives were ushered into Tony's office, where they would lie in wait. Tony gave them a key so they could lock themselves in until they were called upon, and not risk being discovered.

Brian was the first to arrive. He was his customary ten minutes early. Tony greeted him at the front door and directed him to go through to the conference room. Rachel arrived next, with Karina close behind, looking thoroughly put out. 'Is this going to take long? I've got supper in the oven,' she grumbled.

'No, not long, I promise,' said Tony as he closed the door behind them. Once they were on their way upstairs, he locked the door as per Hodge's instructions.

The three new arrivals took up their usual seats around the rectangular conference table, and Tony waited by the conference room door.

Brian leaned back in his chair and held the back of his hand against the insulated coffee jug, which sat on a tray of upturned cups. 'Has no one put a brew on?'

'We're not going to be here too long,' said Tony.

'I don't mind making the coffees, Tony,' said Rachel.

'I haven't brought any milk in, and we're not going to be long.'

'And I've got supper on,' Karina added. 'I like to have it on the table at eight sharp.'

'Aye, so I've heard,' said Brian, chuckling at his own joke. Karina glowered at him. 'You and your filthy mouth.'

'That's enough, thank you,' said Tony.

'Is Leeanne not joining us?' asked Rachel.

'If she knows what's good for her, she won't,' said Karina.

As Tony opened his mouth to answer, Leeanne walked in. 'Hiya,' she said brightly.

Karina's face soured. Leeanne sat down opposite her and smiled at her defiantly.

'Ahem.' Leeanne looked up. 'Have you anything to say for yourself?' asked Karina, the memory of the incident at the church being the real reason she was in a less than sunny mood.

'What? I just said hello when I walked in,' said Leeanne

innocently, fully aware of what the receptionist was referring to.

Then Verity walked in.

'You! What are you doing here?' asked Karina. Verity blanked her and went to take the seat to Leeanne's left. Leeanne stopped her and shook her head. 'That was Naomi's seat,' she said, patting the seat of the chair to her right. Verity took it.

Seeking an explanation for this madness, Karina turned to Tony. 'What's she doing here? She's no right being here. She's not one of us—she tried to kill me!'

'Excuse me?' said Verity, starting to rise. 'You attacked me!'

'That's enough!' Tony said, startling everyone present with a rare display of assertiveness—himself included. 'Please! After everything we've been through in the last few days.' The women settled down, their anger disappearing like a popped balloon. 'Let's remember why we're here and keep this civil.'

'Why are we here? And why is she here?' asked Rachel.

'We're here to have an open and honest chat about the passing of Carl and Naomi, and discuss how we can honour the memory of our friends.'

'On the phone, you said this was about how we come back into the office,' said Brian testily.

'I've asked Verity along because she's been affected by this too, and we'll be talking about returning to work later.'

Rachel got up and made her way to the door.

Tony looked at his watch. 'We're about to start,' he said in a low voice.

Rachel leaned into him and whispered, close enough that he could feel her breath on his neck. 'Sorry. Nature calls.' She slipped past him into the corridor.

'She barely knew either of them,' said Brian.

Rachel reappeared briefly. 'From what I've heard, she knew

them well enough to be accused of murdering them,' she said, lighting the proverbial firework before retiring to a safe distance.

Tony took to his chair, reeling from what Rachel had said. 'Is that true?'

'Of course it's not true,' said Verity indignantly. 'I wasn't charged with anything; I was arrested on suspicion of murdering Naomi simply because I was one of the last people to see her alive. I walked out of the police station a few hours later, without any charges being made.'

'Pssh! There's no smoke without fire,' said Karina.

Tony gave her a withering glare. Rachel returned and took the long way back to her chair to avoid Verity. She sat down and started picking at her cuticles.

'And what about Carl? Did they arrest you for that too?' asked Brian.

'No,' said Verity flatly.

Brian turned to Rachel. 'I thought you said that they'd accused her of murdering both of them?'

Rachel shrugged. 'I don't know. I'm just saying what I'd heard, that's all.'

Brian shook his head. 'We all hear things, but it doesn't necessarily make them true, girl.'

Rachel gave a disinterested shrug and carried on picking at her nails.

Brian directed his question to Verity. 'Did the police say anything about Carl? Are they treating it as murder or what?'

'That's a very good question, Brian,' said Verity, standing up and pushing her chair in. 'Was Carl Donahue murdered?' She began to walk behind them as she talked. 'To answer that, we have to ask ourselves why someone would murder him—or more precisely, why would one of us want to murder him? If he was murdered.' She stopped behind Tony's chair and put her hands on the backrest. 'What about you, Tony?'

'What about me?' he replied uneasily.

'Why would you want to murder Carl?'

Tony twisted in his seat so he could see Verity. 'I didn't murder him!'

'Hypothetically, I mean.'

'I wouldn't. I wouldn't murder anyone.'

'He owed you money—several thousand pounds, I believe.'

'I know—and everyone here knows that too.'

'And he was behind with his payments, wasn't he?'

'Yes, but was only a few hundred pounds.'

'Five hundred pounds, you said. Not an insignificant amount to some people.'

'True, but I've just spent more than that on a pair of shoes.'

Brian looked at him scornfully. 'More money than bloody sense.'

Verity continued. 'But what if it wasn't about the amount at all—what if it was the principle? And when you chased him up those stairs, you got into a row about the money, and you saw you had the perfect opportunity, and in a fit of rage, you lashed out and pushed him?'

'Don't be so ridiculous. I wasn't even in the room when he fell!'

She put her mouth to his ear. 'So you say,' she said softly.

She moved on to Brian, much to Tony's relief.

'And what about you, Brian?'

Brian closed his eyes.

'You and Carl were rivals in love, were you not?'

Verity caught a glimpse of Karina hanging her head.

'That's water under a very old bridge, love,' he said, glancing up at his former lover.

'You know what they say about revenge, don't you?'

'Don't talk rot, woman.'

'A dish best served cold. And what's colder than pushing a man to his death, years after you lost the woman you loved to him?'

Brian bristled at this. Verity moved on to Rachel.

'Why would Rachel want to murder Carl?'

'You're not very good at this, are you? How could I have murdered him? I was on the phone downstairs when it happened, and the police have already checked that.'

'So I'm led to believe, but hypothetically speaking, what reason could you have to kill him?'

'Killing him—none. I can think of one or two for killing you though.'

Verity sidestepped her ominous remark. 'He did try it on with you at the Christmas party, didn't he?'

'Are you for real?' said Rachel. 'It was a drunken kiss at a party. Every woman here'd be in prison if you killed a bloke for doing that.'

'What if it wasn't the first time he'd done it? And what if it wasn't the last? Perhaps you were blackmailing him? That could explain why he was struggling to pay Tony back.'

'I didn't blackmail anyone, you stupid cow!'

Verity stepped away. 'You seem quite angry, given that you couldn't have possibly murdered him.'

'Well, what do you expect? I don't like being accused of stuff I didn't do.'

'I know the feeling,' said Verity. 'And what about you, Karina?'

'Don't you dare say another word!' Karina said, swivelling her chair to track Verity.

'Or what? Are you going to assault me again, in front of all these witnesses?'

'Someone ruddy well ought to,' said Karina.

'Really? Your husband, perhaps. He's an angry man, isn't he?'

'Only when idiots like you provoke him.'

'What if he'd found out you were having an affair with Carl?'

'Are you seriously suggesting my Dennis killed him? Pretty impressive considering that he was at work, eleven miles away!'

Karina turned to the others. 'Why are we listening to this nonsense? If anyone had it in for Carl, it was her! I saw it with my own eyes—her threatening to kill him.'

'It's okay,' said Tony softly. 'Let's hear what she has to say.'

Karina turned back to Verity. 'I don't care what the police think, I know what I saw, and you're not going to convince me otherwise.'

'That's fine. Like I said, this is all hypothetical. So, it's not your husband, but what about you? What if you and Carl had rekindled that old flame, and arranged to meet in the storeroom to stoke the fire, as it were?'

'With my hips? I don't think so. And don't you think you can take the spotlight off yourself by shining it on us, either. Besides, everyone would have seen me going up those stairs.'

Verity smiled. 'Not if you used the fire escape, which runs directly from the storeroom to the fire exit behind reception. Seventeen steps—I counted them earlier.'

All eyes turned to Karina.

'Don't be looking at me. I didn't do it!' she said indignantly.

'As you said yourself, "there's no smoke without fire".'

Verity moved along to the next person at the table.

'Leeanne,' she said, patting her friend on the back.

'Hello,' said Leeanne.

'Why might you want to murder Carl Donahue?'

'Well, he wasn't very nice to Brian, for a start, and he

217

wasn't very nice to Karina, either. He used to say mean things about Tony behind his back, and sometimes to his front. He was a sexist creep, and I didn't like the way he looked at the other girls. He was rude to a lot of people who didn't deserve it. He used to pinch everyone's food out of the fridge, and he used to tease me about my clothes a lot, until I pointed out that he'd worn the same shirt for a week, and he smelled like a steak pie.'

Verity hadn't expected Leeanne to embrace this so fully.

'Thanks for that, Leeanne. Certainly, a lot of reasons there to dislike Carl, but I'm not sure I can see a motive for murder amongst them.'

By now Verity had had completed her lap of the table. She addressed the group. 'And what about me? What reason could I have for killing him?'

A few puzzled expressions blossomed around the room.

'I'd never met the man before in my life, but I don't deny that I had a blazing row with him just a few moments before he died. And as Karina says, I certainly threatened him, but only in the same way we've all threatened to kill someone. If I'd have delivered on those threats, the bodies would be piled high. But I never have, and I don't imagine I ever will.'

To Verity's surprise, she was shocked to see a few heads nodding in agreement with her. Curiosity had got the better of them, and she had their attention.

'But we're forgetting someone, aren't we?' She pointed to the vacant chair to Leeanne's left, and said in a solemn tone, 'What about Naomi?'

'Don't you go speaking ill of the dead, now,' said Brian, his voice laced with foreboding.

'It's not the dead I fear, Brian, it's the living. So, what reason could Naomi have for killing Carl? Perhaps she'd been blackmailing Carl—it was no secret that she was struggling for money. But I guess we'll never know.' She paused a moment to allow her words to sink in. 'After considering all of that, I can see no definitive motive for murder.' She shrugged. 'Maybe he did just trip, and that's all there is to it.'

Confident that she still held the room, she continued.

'But Naomi's different—we know she was murdered. Initially, the police thought I'd killed her, as you know. And I thought Tony had done it, as I'd seen him walking to Naomi's with a bunch of flowers as I left her house—the same flowers I found in her bin this morning.'

Verity walked over to Tony and placed a hand on his shoulder. 'In fact, I was sure he'd murdered Carl, too—with poison, but it turned out to be nothing more than tooth-whitening gel, which explains Tony's dazzling smile.' As if on cue, Tony smiled and immediately felt like an idiot.

With one hand still resting on Tony's shoulder, Verity pulled open the conference room door, and called out into the corridor, 'When you're ready.' A short silence was broken by the sound of a key in a lock, a door opening on dry hinges, and two pairs of footsteps on the warped wooden floorboards. Detectives Hodge and Yates came into the room. Absurdly, Hodge was holding an insulated shopping bag in one gloved hand and a sandwich box in the other. 'Evening, all,' he said, giving Verity a nod. He held up the plastic lunchbox. 'Does anyone fancy a sandwich?'

'But Tony didn't murder Naomi or Carl, did he, Rachel?'

Rachel blanched. With all the confidence in the world, Verity approached the panic-stricken woman.

'Meadows…' said Hodge, his tone indicating she should be careful.

Verity waved away his warning.

'What are you asking me for?' Rachel said, stumbling out of her chair, 'I didn't murder anyone!'

'Oh, I'm afraid you did, Rachel.'

'Liar!' she screamed as tears streaked her contorted face.

'Carl wasn't pushed to his death, but you could say he "tripped", because when he went through that window he was off his head on LSD, which you'd unwittingly given to him.'

'It was his own stupid fault! Naomi was supposed to take it, not him,'

'I don't get it. Why would you want to give Naomi drugs?' asked Tony.

'Just so she'd mess up her interview, that's all. I only used a little bit!'

'So you did all this just to help your chances of getting the job?' said Tony.

'I don't really think this was about the job,' said Verity. 'I think this was about you.'

'Me?' said Tony, his brow a sea of creases. 'Oh, God, please don't tell me she's fallen in love with me,' Tony said, rubbing his forehead.

'No, I don't think she's in love with you, but I do think she's in love with the *idea* of being in love with you,' said Verity.

'What's that supposed to mean?' asked Tony.

'I think she saw you as a way out.'

'A way out of what?'

'Out of her father's house, out of her old life, and into yours,' said Verity.

'And how was that supposed to work, exactly?' asked Tony.

'I think that once she got the job, she hoped to turn on the charm and turn your head.'

'She'd have to do more than turn my head,' said Tony. 'Is that right, Rachel?'

Rachel snivelled and nodded without looking up.

'Talk about barking up the wrong tree,' he said, shaking his head in utter disbelief.

Brian gave Tony a curious look. 'What's that supposed to mean?'

'What do you think it means, Brian?' said Tony.

'Well, I dunno—oh. Oh, okay, I'm with you,' said Brian. 'Fair play to you.'

Hodge pulled out a pair of handcuffs and weighed them in the palm of his hand for a moment, before handing them to Yates. 'Go on. You can do the honours.'

Yates took the cuffs. 'Cheers, boss.'

In the last few seconds, people had become lost in a rolling tide of emotions.

'Err. Help?' said Verity meekly, finding it difficult to talk with the pointy end of a fountain pen pressed into her neck.

'Whoa! Let's not do anything hasty now,' said Yates, placing the handcuffs in her jacket pocket and showing Rachel empty hands.

'Stay away from me!' Rachel said, using Verity as a shield. Everyone in the room froze.

Tears rolled down Rachel's cheeks and her chin quivered before the dam gave way to the weight of her guilt, and her confession gushed out of her.

'I didn't murder anyone, I swear! I found some acid at home, in my dad's caravan. How was I supposed to know Carl would take it? And Naomi must have found out what had happened 'cos she sent me a message saying, "I know you killed Carl" and she said she wanted five grand, or she was going to the police. I told her I didn't do anything, so she sent me the video. I got money out of my savings, but there was only a few hundred quid, and I went to see her to give her that. On the way, I saw Tony leaving her house, so I turned away so he couldn't see me. When I got there, I saw he'd given her flowers and then she started saying that Tony wouldn't fancy me and then she wanted ten grand by next week or else, so I smashed the flowers, and she started screaming at me to get out and calling me a murderer and that. Then she ran upstairs, so I went after her and she just carried on, so I pushed her to shut her up and the next thing she's at the bottom of the stairs, not moving or anything. I panicked and cleaned up the flowers and got out. I would have called an ambulance, I swear, but it was too late. It was an accident, that's all, just a stupid accident.'

Yates began to move forward. 'Okay, Rachel, I understand—'

'Get back!' she said, jamming the pen nib into Verity's neck. 'Stay away from me or I'm going to make a lot of mess on this carpet.'

The group backed away, moving steadily toward the corner of the room as Rachel advanced with her hostage.

'How about a cup of tea?' said Leeanne.

Rachel stopped dead, baffled by the absurdity of the question. 'You what?' Her concentration lapsed for a scant second, and in that instant, Leeanne struck, kicking Naomi's chair at Rachel, who threw out an arm to defend herself. Fuelled by adrenaline, Verity pulled free of her captor and shot past Leeanne, who was travelling at speed in the opposite direction. Leeanne pounced on Rachel and, in a blur of movement, Rachel was taken to the floor, hard, her arms now locked behind her like a well-trussed chicken, Leeanne pinned her down with a knee and controlled her with a joint-wrenching wrist lock. 'I don't like you very much!' said Leeanne, as she applied a little more pressure to Rachel's wrist, causing her to drop the pen and cry out in pain.

The second Verity was out of danger and Rachel was subdued, Yates rushed forward and snapped the cuffs on

Rachel, cautioning her as she did so. Once Rachel was secured and arrested, Yates hoisted her to her feet and began marching her toward the door.

'No, wait, please!' said Rachel. Hodge stood aside, letting Yates and her prisoner past. He gave Verity a nod of acknowledgment before joining his colleague, as she escorted Rachel out of the building and into the waiting police van.

In the days that followed the arrest of Rachel Eaves, life began to return to normal for most of the residents of Hawbury, all except for three families—two who were preparing to bury their loved ones, and a third preparing to see their only child imprisoned for murder.

As the weekend loomed, Verity made her first real effort to reintegrate into society by walking into the village to buy groceries and some bits and pieces to brighten up the cottage. She was just unpacking the last of her bags when there was a knock at her front door. She folded her newly acquired Hawbury tea towel and draped it over the oven door handle, before answering the door.

She was surprised to find Hodge standing there.

'Evening, Meadows,' said Hodge cheerily.

'Did you not see the sign?'

'What sign?'

'The one that says, "no hawkers, no religious bodies, and no riffraff".'

Hodge responded with a short, mirthless laugh. 'Oh, Meadows, you do crack me up. Now, are you going to invite me in or what?'

'I don't think so. I've only just had the place fumigated after your last visit.'

'Ouch. Even if I come with a peace offering?' said Hodge, holding out a black plastic carrier bag.

Verity was reluctant to take the bag, but curiosity got the better of her. She peered into it gingerly, as though she were half expecting it to explode. It contained four cans of strong Belgian lager, a lukewarm pie, and a four-pack of jam doughnuts.

'You really shouldn't have, Detective. Really,' she said, handing the bag back to him.

'Suit yourself,' he said, cracking open one of the cans and taking a long swig.

Verity looked aghast. 'I take it you're not on duty?'

'Nope,' he said, issuing a long, foamy belch.

Verity looked suitably disgusted.

'I take it you're not here to try to pin another murder on me?'

'Nope. Nothing of the sort. I just came to apologise.'

'Apologise for what, exactly? Falsely accusing me of murder, twice, digging into my private life, or generally just being an insufferable swine?'

'Hey, that's not fair. I only arrested you on suspicion of one murder, and given the circumstances, you would have done the same in my position.'

'No, Detective. If I were in your position, I would have arrested the right person in the first place.'

Hodge held his hands up. 'Alright, nobody's perfect, Meadows. But we got it right in the end, didn't we?'

'Oh, *we* did, did we?'

'Your contribution to the case was invaluable, no question.'

Though understated, the detective's acknowledgment of her role in solving this case gave Verity an unexpected thrill.

'But I'd rather we didn't make a habit of this in future, all the same,' said Hodge.

'The feeling's mutual, I can assure you,' said Verity. 'Tell me, how's the case progressing?'

'Good. We're going for murder on both counts, but with decent representation, I wouldn't be surprised if it gets knocked down to manslaughter,' said Hodge.

'Still, even if it does, she's going to be looking at a lengthy sentence, I assume?'

'Ten to twelve years, maybe. Out in six,' said Hodge, as he drained the last of the lager.

'Really? As little as that?'

'Yep. Not much, is it? Three years for a life.'

'No, it's not,' said Verity. 'You don't think she would come back here, do you?'

'Unlikely. She'll probably change her name and move halfway across the country—you know how it goes,' he said, raising an eyebrow at Verity.

'Right,' he said, crumpling his empty can and dropping it into his carrier bag. 'I'll be seeing you.'

'Not anytime soon, I hope,' she said.

'And not in a professional capacity, next time, eh?' said Hodge, as he turned and walked away.

'Oh, Detective,' said Verity.

Hodge turned back.

'What?'

'You can leave the doughnuts,' she said, with a hint of a smile.

EPILOGUE

Leeanne called round to see Verity a week later. After attending two funerals back to back, they were both keen to find something to lift their spirits, and Leeanne believed she'd found just the thing.

'Good news,' she said as she came skipping into Verity's kitchen, not bothering to knock. 'I've got two tickets to the Hawbury Players' legendary Murder Mystery evening in a few weeks.'

'I see. And these "players" are an am dram group, I take it?'

'Yeah, that's right.'

'Do you know what I'd like more than watching an am dram performance?' said Verity.

'I dunno?'

'Not watching an am dram performance.'

Leeanne made a face. 'Oh, don't be like that. They're always good for a giggle. I'd take Gary, but he just ends up getting drunk and shouting, "The butler did it!", because the first year we went to it he shouted it and it turned out he was right. But it wasn't the butler the last five times we've been, so I thought you'd like to come instead?'

Verity considered it. She'd had quite enough of actual murders for a while, but it might be nice to just play at being a detective for a change, without the risk of getting arrested.

'And what's the name of this "legendary" performance?'

Leeanne pulled a crumpled leaflet out of her back pocket and consulted it. 'It's called "Murder Most Deadly".'

'Murder Most Deadly? Well, it can't be any worse than the title, I suppose,' said Verity.

'Oh, come on, it'll be a laugh.'

'And when you say it'll be a laugh, will we be laughing with them or at them?'

'Oh, at them, definitely,' said Leeanne.

Verity had to admit that she did rather like the sound of that.

'All right,' she said, taking the leaflet from Leeanne and reading it. 'What's the worst that could happen?'

THE END

JOIN THE READERS' CLUB

Dear Reader,

Thank you for choosing this book. I hope you enjoyed reading it as much as I enjoyed writing it. If you did, I'd love it if you could take a moment to leave a quick review on Amazon, as these help me reach new readers.

I love to stay in touch with my readers, so I occasionally send out newsletters with details of new releases, special offers, competitions, events, and other book-related news.

By subscribing to my newsletter, you'll also have a chance to appear in one of my future novels (I'll be gentle with you, I promise!). To sign up, please visit my website. I hope to see you there.

AJFordWrites.Com

ABOUT THE AUTHOR

A J Ford dreams of living in a café-cum-bookshop by the sea and spending their days writing crime novels on an old-fashioned typewriter. You can find out more about the author by following them on Twitter or visiting their website: AJFordWrites.com.

For more information, please email:
ajfordwrites@gmail.com

 twitter.com/AJFordWrites

Printed in Poland
by Amazon Fulfillment
Poland Sp. z o.o., Wrocław

84108584R00141